David Walliams

SLIME

Illustrated by Tony Ross

HarperCollins *Children's Books*

First published in the United Kingdom by
HarperCollins *Children's Books* in 2020
Published in this paperback edition in 2022
HarperCollins *Children's Books* is a division
of HarperCollins*Publishers* Ltd
1 London Bridge Street
London SE1 9GF

www.harpercollins.co.uk

HarperCollins*Publishers*
1st Floor, Watermarque Building, Ringsend Road
Dublin 4, Ireland

1

ISBN 978-0-00-840955-5

For Dante,
the coolest kid on wheels

This story is set on the Isle of Mulch. The little island is home to some big characters...

Meet **NED**. Ned is a bright and funny boy of eleven. Because his legs haven't worked since he was a baby, Ned uses a wheelchair to whizz around Mulch.

JEMIMA is Ned's older sister. Jemima likes nothing more than playing the most horrid tricks on her little brother.

NED'S PARENTS: Dad spends all day on his fishing boat out at sea. Mum spends all day at the island's market selling the fish he catches.

SIR WALTER WRATH is the headmaster of Ned's old school, Mulch School for Revolting Children. It is the boy's old school because Sir Walter expelled Ned in one of his notorious volcanic rages.

MR LUST is the deputy head of Mulch School for Revolting Children. Day and night he lusts after the top job, that of headmaster.

EDMUND and **EDMOND ENVY** run the only toyshop on the island, named Envy's Emporium. The terrible twins loathe children for the simple crime of being young, and send the poor mites fleeing from their shop in floods of tears.

MADAME SOLENZIO SLOTH is the world's laziest piano teacher. The lady is paid good money to give piano lessons to children. However, all she does is snooze on the sofa as she blows off. THUNDEROUSLY.

CAPTAIN PRIDE is the island's park keeper. The public park is the ex-army officer's pride and joy. So much so that absolutely no one is ever allowed to set foot inside it. Especially not nasty little children who will trample his precious grass.

GLEN and **GLENDA GLUTTON** own the only ice-cream van on the island, Glutton's Glaces. That is because they have rammed all their rival ice-cream vans off the road. The married couple are thieves who snatch children's pocket money, and then speed off without giving them their ice creams. Instead, the evil pair scoff all the ice cream themselves.

AUNT GRETA GREED is Ned and Jemima's mega-rich auntie. She owns the Isle of Mulch. The grand old lady lives alone in a castle high on a hill that overlooks the entire island. All she has to keep her company are more than a hundred cats, all called Tiddles.

GIGANTIC TIDDLES is Aunt Greta's heftiest cat. It is the size and weight of a bear, and infinitely more fearsome.

And last but not least, **SLIME**.

Oh yes, Slime is very much alive. It is a creature with powers to change shape or "trans-slime" into ANYTHING and EVERYTHING.

But is Slime a force for
GOOD or EVIL?
You must read on...

RAJ the newsagent does not live on Mulch.

Prologue

A BRIEF
HISTORY OF
SLIME

SLIME is one of the greatest mysteries of the world. If not

STONEHENGE

the greatest. It beats the creation of Stonehenge, laughs in the face of the power of the pyramids and

THE PYRAMIDS

takes a giant slimy plop on the Loch Ness Monster.

SLIME.

What is it?

Where is it?

Who is it?

How is it?

And why is it?

THE LOCH NESS MONSTER

SLIME

Children demand to know where SLIME came from. And grown-ups are desperate to know if it is ever going back.

For the first time in history, the legend of SLIME can finally be told. All will be revealed in this book, which might be the most important book ever writtened.*

Some experts believe that SLIME dates back billions of years.

Their theory is that when the Earth was created it was nothing more than a sea of SLIME. Out of that SLIME came more SLIME. And out of that slime came more SLIME. Then, of course, out of that SLIME came even more SLIME. It remained buried under the Earth for billions of years. Until now...

Others suppose that at the dawn of time a giant meteor of SLIME crash-landed into the Earth. On impact, billions of gallons of SLIME exploded into the air, covering every living thing in thick SLIME. This explains why the dinosaurs died out. They got SLIMED.

---

* A real word you will find in your Walliamsictionary, the world's number-one dictionary.

There is another theory that many years ago

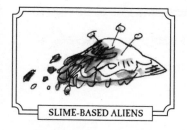

SLIME-BASED ALIENS

SLIME-based aliens from a SLIME-based planet (the planet SLIME) flew in a SLIME-based spaceship to the Earth. Once on Earth they taught ancient civilisations all about SLIME.

How to construct buildings out of SLIME.

The best recipes to cook with SLIME.

And, most importantly, how to make socks out of SLIME.

Then the SLIME-based aliens got in their SLIME-based spaceship

SLIME BUILDINGS

and whizzed back to their SLIME-based planet, the planet SLIME. And they never came again. But they left the secret of SLIME with the human race, so children could torment grown-ups with it forever.

The truth is rather different.

SLIME was actually created more than fifty years

ago on a remote island. The ISLE OF MULCH, to be precise. It is situated in the middle of the Great Northeastsouthwestern Sea, between the islands of Twaddle and Stench.

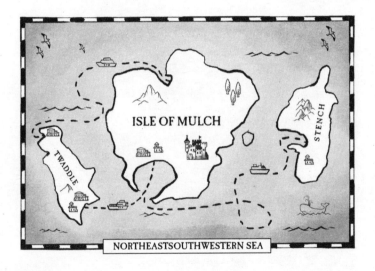

ISLE OF MULCH

TWADDLE

STENCH

NORTHEASTSOUTHWESTERN SEA

How do I know all this?
Because I just made it up.

MAP OF THE ISLE OF MULCH

Madame Solenzio Sloth's home

Envy's Emporium

Ned's family home

Market

Port

Sea

Chapter 1

MULCH

The little **ISLE OF MULCH** was home to less than a thousand people, **999** to be precise. I told you it was less than a thousand.

One of these **999** people was a boy named Ned. "Ned" wasn't short for anything – he was just called Ned. Ned was eleven years old. He'd been born on **MULCH** and, like most islanders, had never left.

To say Ned was just an ordinary boy would be wrong. He wasn't ORDINARY – he was **extraordinary**. Ned had been born with legs that didn't work. He couldn't walk at all, so was found a battered old rusty wheelchair and he learned to use it. The boy could often be seen whizzing around the island, doing stunts and wheelies to delight his friends.

"I got the *ZOOMIES!*"

he would cry as he whizzed past.

Home for Ned was a tiny weather-beaten old cottage. The cottage perched on the edge of a cliff overlooking the raging sea that surrounded the island.

From dawn until dusk, Ned's mother and father were out of the house at work. Dad was a fisherman, so was away at sea all day on his fishing boat. Mum sold the fish Dad caught at the island's market. The only fish you could catch around the **ISLE OF MULCH** were called shoe fish. They were fish shaped like shoes.

SHOE FISH

SHOE

They tasted like shoes too. The overriding flavour was foot sweat. But the locals became used to the taste, disgusting though it was. They had no choice.

Needless to say, both Ned's parents absolutely STANK of fish. But Ned didn't see or even smell much of them as the pair were always working.

Instead, the boy was left home alone with his older sister. Jemima resented Ned deeply. She might have been the older one, but it was her younger brother who got all the attention.

The girl wore pretty little *flowery* dresses, with huge **STEEL-CAPPED** boots, and she wasn't afraid to use them.

Mulch

Ned's aunt owned the **ISLE OF MULCH**. She was his mother's much older sister, and her name was Greta Greed. High on a hill overlooking the whole island squatted **KITTY LITTER CASTLE** – a huge medieval fortress that the lady called home. It was a world away from the tiny cottage that Ned shared with his family.

Greed lived there alone, which is how she liked it. Her only company was her 101 cats. These cats were fearsome beasts… She had them to scare nasty little children away.

The lady loathed children, especially her poor nephew, Ned. Aunt Greta never, ever did a thing to help him. For her, children ruined her **ISLE OF MULCH** with their games, their chatter and, worst of all, their stench. Aunt Greta should be the last person to complain about a smell as she stank of cat pee.

Because **Aunt Greta** owned the entire island, she had power over all those who lived there. The lady rewarded those grown-ups on Mulch who detested children almost as much as she did.

One such man was **Sir Walter Wrath.** He was a nasty old wretch whom Greed had made headmaster of the only school on the island, Mᴜʟᴄʜ Sᴄʜᴏᴏʟ ғᴏʀ Rᴇᴠᴏʟᴛɪɴɢ Cʜɪʟᴅʀᴇɴ. The only thing that gave Wrath pleasure was expelling children from his school. Like so many others, Ned had suffered that fate.

There was one toyshop on the island. Greed had given care of it to twin brothers. **Edmund and Edmond Envy** had named the shop Eɴᴠʏ's Eᴍᴘᴏʀɪᴜᴍ,

but it was nothing more than a front for terrorising children. Ned had had a particularly nasty time when he'd last visited.

Another resident of Mulch was **Madame Solenzio Sloth.** The lady was supposed to be a piano teacher, but she was too lazy to teach children anything. Sloth was a virtuoso of cruelty. Ned had the misfortune of

being one of her pupils, and when he'd dared to complain all hell broke loose.

Captain Pride was an uptight ex-soldier whom Greed had appointed Mulch's park keeper. The captain ensured no one could ever enjoy the island's only public park,

especially not little people like Ned.

Ice-cream sellers **Glen and Glenda Glutton** made sure children never got to enjoy an ice cream, ever. The married couple *zoomed* around the island in their van, looking for children to rob. They took their pocket money,

and then sped off without giving them their ice cream. If the Gluttons had lived anywhere else in the world, other than **MULCH,** they would have been locked up in prison and the key thrown away. However, Greed delighted in their scam, and ensured the pair were never brought to justice, even when they stole from her own nephew, Ned.

So this little island was home to a large number of horrible grown-ups. But there was a child on the island who was probably as bad.

Poor Ned was related to her.

It was his sister.

Chapter 2
A BEASTLY GIRL

Ned's sister, Jemima, liked nothing more than playing horrid tricks on her little brother. Tricks that made the girl snigger to herself all day and all night.

"TEE! HEE! HEE!"

It wasn't a nice snigger. It was a **nasty** snigger, as if she knew she was beastly.

The tricks were all absolutely foul:

Dropping wiggly-waggly worms down the back of her little brother's pyjamas.

"YIKES!"

Replacing Ned's toothpaste with glue so his teeth stuck together.

"MMM!"

Emptying the jar of his favourite marmalade and replacing it with mashed-up wasps.

"YUCK!"

Painting everything in her little brother's room bright purple – the walls, the floor, the ceiling, his toys and clothes, even his pet gerbil.

"NOOOO!"

Hiding a big **furry** spider at the end of his bed so it nibbled his toes.

"ARGH!" "YOW!"

Dusting the toilet seat with chilli powder so the boy's botty was too, too hotty.

Swapping Ned's favourite chocolate-coated raisins with gerbil droppings.
"EURGH!"

Breaking wind into an old wooden box for a week. Then opening it in Ned's bedroom so he would suffer the PONGTASMAGORIA.*
"POOOOOOOOOOOO!"
However, all this was nothing compared to the nightmarish trick Jemima was planning for her little brother.

* *Another real word you will find with ease in your* Walliamsictionary.

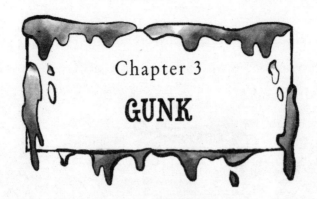

Chapter 3
GUNK

Jemima was a child who revelled in all things
JYUCKY. Not just spiders and worms,
but **GOOEY** things too. All around the little
cottage where the family lived, the girl had
hidden **gunk** in jars.

Things you found under rocks. Things you
found at the bottom of ponds. Things you
found lurking down the plughole.

Jemima would scoop up anything nasty and
deposit it in a jar. Over time, she had collected
hundreds and hundreds of jars of all
different kinds of **gunk.** Every single one had
a label on it so Jemima could remember what
was what. One shudders to think how the girl

collected some of these revolting things. You would not want to touch this stuff with your bare hands!

At the bottom of every wardrobe, at the back of every cupboard, under the floorboards, there were jars and jars and more jars.

Jemima was stockpiling them in the family cottage, as she wanted to play the most **HUMONGOUS** trick on her little brother.

A trick that would make him scream the house down.

"AAAAARRRRRGGGGGHHHHH!"

A scream that would echo all over the **ISLE OF MULCH** forever.

Jemima would snigger herself to sleep thinking about her devilish plan.

"TEE! *HEE!* HEE!"

There was just one problem.

Her little brother was on to her.

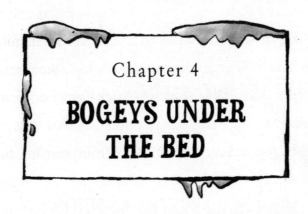

Chapter 4

BOGEYS UNDER THE BED

Ned found the jars. Just one jar at first. In a deep sleep, Ned had rolled off his bed in the dead of night.

THUD!

"OUCH!"

The fall woke him up. Just as he was about to haul himself back up, Ned noticed something glinting in the darkness under his bed.

He reached out and found it was a jar. The label – in his sister's scrawled handwriting – read simply **BOGEYS**. On closer inspection, he discovered it really was a jar bursting with **bogeys**. They looked very much like Jemima's. She had picked, **licked** and *flicked* so many at Ned over the years that he could recognise them in any line-up in an instant. Hers were always a brownish shade of green.

At once Ned knew his wicked sister was up to something.

But why had she hidden her own **bogeys** in a jar under his bed?

Lifting up the sheets, he saw that this was just one of what must have been a hundred jars under there… each containing something more disgusting than the last. Ned's eyes b u l g e d as he read the labels.

GROUND ANTS

BOILED DANDRUFF

YELLOW PUS

BROWN PUS

YELLOWY BROWN PUS

SLOBBER

BROWNY YELLOW PUS

SLUDGE FOUND DOWN THE PLUGHOLE AFTER A BATH

CHEESY BURPS

MEATY BURPS

SPICY BURPS

WART SOUP

BURPY BURPS

MONKEY SWEAT

TOAD JUICE

Ten-year-old trifle that has gone so fizzy it will BLOW YOUR HEAD OFF

PUDDLE GUNGE OR "PUNGE"*

Something even more UNSPEAKABLE than the other UNSPEAKABLE thing that cannot ever be named

*This is the correct word. If in any doubt, please check your Walliamsictionary, the best source of made-up words in the world.

One by one, Ned pulled all the jars out from under his bed. He was careful not to clink them together. The sound would wake up his wicked sister, who was sleeping in her room next door.

Then Ned hoisted himself up on to his battered old wheelchair so he could go hunting for more jars.

One good thing about getting around on wheels is that you can glide silently and undetected.

As long as you don't bump into the furniture.

DONK!

Or run over a cat.

"MIAow!"

Ned rolled past his sister's bedroom and headed into the living room. *Now*, thought Ned, *where would be good hiding places?*

It turned out… everywhere!

There were jars, jars and more jars of yucktastic* stuff hidden all over the room.

---

* *Don't delay. Buy your* Walliamsictionary *today.*

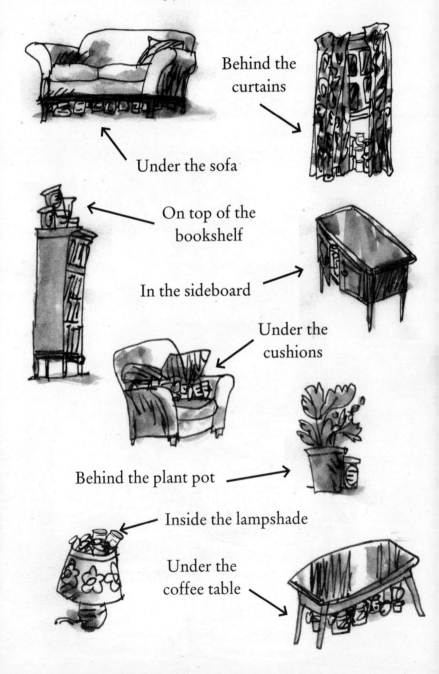

Behind the
curtains

Under the sofa

On top of the
bookshelf

In the sideboard

Under the
cushions

Behind the plant pot

Inside the lampshade

Under the
coffee table

The same was true of the kitchen. And the hallway.

Rolling past the boiler cupboard, Ned heard gurgling.

GURGLE! FURGLE! DURGLE!

On opening the door, he could see jars and jars with **gunk** oozing out of them. The heat from the boiler must have made the **gunk** expand. It was a wonder that one of the jars hadn't exploded.

Once again, all the jars were labelled, each full of something more puzzling than the last.

What was all this stuff?

And, more importantly, what was
she planning to do with it all?

The boy approached his mother and father's room. He peeked through the gap in the door. Their bed was empty. It was the early hours of the morning and the pair were already at work. No doubt Dad was heading out to sea and Mum was setting up her market stall. A quick search by Ned of the back of their wardrobe revealed jars, jars and more jars.

"Curiouser and curiouser," he muttered to himself.

Then the boy rolled back into the hall, making his way towards his dreaded sister's bedroom.

TRUNDLE! TRUNDLE! TRUNDLE!

Ned was sure somewhere in there would be the answer. He put his ear up against her door.

"ZZZ! ZZZ! ZZZ!"

Jemima was fast asleep, snoring like a steam train.

The sign on her bedroom door read…

Now was Ned's chance. The boy took a deep breath. Then, as quietly as he could, he opened the door...

CLICK!

...and gently rolled himself inside.

TRUNDLE!

The boy hadn't been allowed in his sister's bedroom for years. No wonder she kept everyone out. Her room was full to bursting with jars and jars and more jars of **gunk!** There must have been thousands upon thousands of jars in there. All the way from

the floor to the ceiling. No wonder Jemima had resorted to hiding the jars all over the house. There was no more room in her room! It was a miracle she could even get in or out!

As Ned watched his sister sleep, noting that she wore her **STEEL-CAPPED** boots in bed, he scanned her bedroom for clues. There must be an answer somewhere to what she planned to do with all these jars of **gunk.**

In a corner of the room were Jemima's school exercise books. Ned knew that his sister never did a scrap of work at school, so was surprised to see how well thumbed the books looked. Upon opening them, Ned discovered that they weren't full of schoolwork at all. Oh no.

They were full of plans for the
diabolical trick she was about
to play on him...

Chapter 5

THE BATH OF DOOM

Ned's eyes widened at the horror. The unspeakable horror.

The words and pictures in her books told the story in gruesome detail.

So this was what his wicked sister was planning!

There were lists, calendars, graphs, diagrams and even a flick book of how it would all play out.

It was called:

And it was the boy's birthday…
TOMORROW!

Once a year on his birthday, Ned had a bath.*

In the family cottage there was only enough hot water for one bathful a day. Of course, Jemima always bagsied every drop of hot water for herself. No wonder her parents **reeked** of fish.

The only exception to this rule was on her little brother's birthday. On that special day, Jemima would be forced by her parents to relent and let little **STINKY** Ned have his yearly soak.

So the plan was that tomorrow Jemima would fill the bath with all the **gunk.** Every last drop from every single jar would be emptied until the bath was full to the brim. Then she would squirt bubbles on top of the **gunk,** so Ned wouldn't see the horror that was lurking underneath.

---

* *I know that doesn't sound like many baths in one year. One. I, myself, like to wash at least twice a year. Unless I am already clean and there is no need. Sometimes I lick myself clean like a cat.*

The Bath of Doom.

There was even a cut-away diagram in her exercise book showing the hidden layer of **gunk.**

Bubbles

Water

Gunk

Jemima knew her little brother would suspect nothing. This was his birthday treat, after all! Ned would think it was a lovely bath full of warm water and lower himself into it. THEN...

"EURGH!" he would scream as he was covered from head to toe in **gunk.**

Ned dropped Jemima's book in shock.

THONK!

The girl stirred.

Ned held his breath.

Then she turned over and went straight back to sleep.

"ZZZ! ZZZZ! ZZZZZ!"

Taking great care, the boy rolled himself back out of Jemima's bedroom. He had to reverse his wheelchair, as with the mountains of jars there wasn't room to turn round.

TRUNDLE! TRUNDLE! TRUNDLE!

Then... DISASTER!

CLUNK! CLINK! CLANK!

The footrest on his wheelchair just clipped one of the jars on the floor. There must have been fifty jars stacked on top of it.

Ned reached out, but he was too late. The skyscraper of jars began toppling over.

TIPPLE! TOPPLE! TUPPLE!

The jar at the top was heading straight for Jemima!

As it fell through the air, it was as if time sped up and slowed down all at once.

SNATCH!

Ned caught the jar just as it was a milli-milli-millimetre from **THUNKING** his sister on the head. As much as he may have wanted to see his sister thunked on the head with a jar of GRUMBLENOSH (whatever that was), sadly now was not the time.

It would spoil *his* surprise!

Because just at that moment an idea came to him.

D I N G !

An idea so simple it was brilliant. Simply brilliant and brilliantly simple. **BRIMPLE.***

Ned would turn the tables on Jemima!

---

* *Consult your* Walliamsictionary *for a detailed definition.*

The girl had a bath every single morning (apart from Ned's birthday, keep up). So Ned would do to her **EXACTLY** what his sister was going to do to him. She would suffer the **Bath of Doom** herself!

Ned silently collected up all the jars of gunk in the house, and brought them to the bathroom.

Once safely inside, Ned locked the door.

CLICK!

He didn't want Jemima bursting in on him before her **Bath of Doom** was ready.

"Ha! Ha!" chuckled the boy to himself.

Outside it was still dark, but dawn was breaking and the birds were bursting into song.

"TWEET! TWEET! TWEET!"

One by one, he opened the jars of **gunk,** and poured them into the bath.

SPLISH! SPLASH!

SPLOSH!

There was...

BROWN gunk

Yellow gunk

Black gunk

THICK gunk

THIN gunk

Purple gunk

FIZZY gunk

HOT gunk

Bubbly gunk

Cold gunk

Every kind of gunk you could imagine.
Gallons and gallons of **gunk**.
Eventually the bath was full.

After what seemed like hours of fetching, carrying and unscrewing, the boy was exhausted. Catching his breath, Ned didn't notice what was happening right behind him.

GURGLE!

Whatever was in that bath was
coming to life…!

Chapter 6

GUNK MONSTER

As all the different types of **gunk** swirled together, waves formed in the bath.

SWISH!

The waves swept up, up, up...

SWASH!

...and they swept down, down, down.

S W U S H !

Ned turned round. It was a horrifying sight. He opened his mouth to scream, but no sound came out.

The bath was now a raging storm of **gunk**.

SWISH! SWASH! SWOOSH!

It splashed all over the bathroom, coating everything in **gunk**.

SPLISH! SPLASH! SPLOSH!

The sink, the toilet, even Ned – all were

GUNKED!

Then, just as soon as the **gunk** had coated everything, it peeled itself off and **whooshed** back together.

WOOMPH!

Then the **gunk** began to take shape.

At first it became a giant egg. Like the kind of egg a dinosaur might have laid. The egg bounced up and down...

BOING! BOING! BOING!

...before smashing itself against the bathroom wall.

CRACK!

The outer layer cracked like a shell as the gunk inside oozed out.

The oozing **gunk** then began to grow upwards and upwards, becoming a mountain.

WHOOSH!

No, it was a volcano!

An erupting volcano!

It didn't shoot lava up into the sky, but, rather, **gunk!**

KABOOM! SPLURT!

It spurted itself all over the bathroom ceiling before oozing back down to the floor to become an elephant.

"HOO!" it hooted.

Then it became a shark!

"CHOMP!"

No, a bird!

FLAP! FLAP!

This gunk monster was
swimming and flying all at once.

SWISH! FLAP! SWISH! FLAP!

The boy gazed open-mouthed in awe.
This was the greatest show on Earth!
And it was all for him!
Next the gunk monster
exploded into thousands of
pieces as it became fireworks.

BOOM!
BOOM!
BOOM!

"Oh no!" exclaimed the boy.
"What on earth
have I done?"

Chapter 7
BLOBBY BLOB

What the boy had done that day changed the course of history.

In mixing together a thousand different jars of **gunk,** Ned had created a brand-new matter.

The world would never be the same again. This was big. Bigger than big. Bigger than biggest. **HUGE-A-MONGOUS!***

---

* It means "big". You would know that if you owned a Walliamsictionary.

As Ned stayed deadly still, the slime began spinning round and round him.

WHIZZ!

It was a **tornado** of slime.

A **SLIMEADO!*

---

* *Open your* **Walliamsictionary** *under "S" for a detailed definition.*

NO! thought Ned. *I am going to be slimed to death.*

He shut his eyes tight, and cried, **"ARGH!"**

Then the most amazing thing happened.

The whirling tube of slime spun up over his head and slapped against the ceiling.

SQUELCH!

Then it began **o o z i n g** downwards towards the boy.

As it did, it began to take shape.

Not human shape exactly.

More like a **blob** on top of a **blob** on top of a **blob**.

It is easier if I show you.

It looked like this…

A **blobby blobulous*** **blob** that was hanging down from the ceiling.

A huge, slimy upside-down face was staring straight back at him.

---

* *The* **Walliams***ictionary definition is "something very, very, very, very, very, VERY blobby".*

"Good morning!" it boomed.

The boy's eyes darted around the bathroom.

There was no one else there.

This thing was talking to him!

"I said, 'Good morning'!" it repeated.

For something made of slime it had a surprisingly posh voice. As if it were royal. Which seemed highly unlikely. Last time I checked, the royal family did not have a member who was made entirely of slime.

"Who are y-y-you?" stammered Ned. The boy was trembling with fear.

"I am anything you want me to be," replied the thing.

With that, the blob of slime squelched upside down across the ceiling.

SQUELCH! SQUELCH! SQUELCH! SQUELCH!

Next, it made its way down the wall, its slimy bottom acting like a suction pad against it.

SQUELCH!
SQUELCH!
SQUELCH!
SQUELCH!

Eventually the thing was standing on the floor of the bathroom, peering down at Ned.

"Now, boy, tell me what you wish me to be."

"Is this like Aladdin?" asked Ned excitedly.

"Is what like Aladdin?"

"Like rubbing the lamp, and a genie coming out, and the genie giving you three wishes?"

The slime looked lost in thought for a moment before replying, **"No. There is no lamp. I am not a genie. And there aren't three wishes."**

"Oh," replied Ned.

"There are infinite wishes!"

"That's a lot, isn't it?"

"It's infinite, so, yes, I suppose it is. Unless it was infinite and one, which would be silly."

"Cool!" exclaimed Ned.

"So, boy, what do you wish me to be? I can be anything and everything!

A hippopotamus! A swarm of bees! A giant pair of bloomers!"

As it spoke, it shapeshifted into each thing. "Just think of something beginning with S! A sailing ship.
A sphinx.

A sausage as tall as a tree. A steamroller…"

The boy looked on in wonder as it changed with dizzying speed.

"A symphony!"

With that, there was the sound of a huge drum being struck.

BOOM!

The slime shattered into what seemed like hundreds of tiny **globules.** They flew past

Ned, and he realised that these weren't just **globules.** They were musical notes! As the sound of a symphony echoed around the bathroom, these musical notes danced through the air like butterflies. The boy watched in awe as they swooped and twirled in time to the music.

"W-w-wow!" he stammered.

Then, just as soon as the symphony ended, the **globules** all merged together. This time they didn't go back into being **Slime's blobulous** self.

Oh no.

The **globules** merged back into the shape of a whale. The whale was so humongous it filled up the entire bathroom.

It floated in the air, swishing its tail.

SWISH! SWUSH! SWOSH!

"**Am I back to normal?**" it asked. "**Something feels fishy.**"

"No! You are not back to normal!" exclaimed Ned. "Unless it is normal for you to be a great big ginormous whale!"

The whale of slime looked down, and then fell through the air.

SPLAT!

It landed like dropped jelly on the bathroom floor.

S I L E N C E.

Ned stared at it. Whatever this thing was, it looked to be no more. It was an ex-thing. Lying motionless next to the wheels of the boy's wheelchair was nothing more than a puddle of **gloop.**

"Slime!" called out Ned. He couldn't think what else to call it, and **"Slime"** seemed appropriate. "Are you all right?"

After a moment, the slime poured itself back together into the shape of a blob.

"That's better," it said. **"I felt all over the place."**

"Thank goodness!" exclaimed Ned.

"Is 'Slime' my name, then?" it asked.

"I can't think of a better one."

"Erm, Roger? Archibald? Brenda?" offered **Slime**. **"I do feel like a Brenda."**

"Mmm," mused the boy. "I think you look more like a **'Slime'**."

"'Slime' it is!" said **Slime**. It gave the boy a funny look, as much as a blob of slime can give anyone a funny look. **"So, did you create me?"**

"Um, well," hesitated Ned, "I guess I did!"

"FATHER!" exclaimed **Slime**.

"No!"

"MOTHER?"

"NO!"

"What, then?"

"I guess we are… well –" Ned didn't dare say it at first, but something in his heart told him he should – "friends."

"Friends," repeated **Slime**. **"Friends! I like that! Yes! We are friends!"**

The boy smiled and leaned over to hug his new friend, but all he got was a face full of slime.

"You didn't tell me your name," remarked **Slime**.

"Ned," replied Ned.

"I have a friend called Ned!" exclaimed **Slime**.

"And, **Slime**?"

"Yes, Ned?"

"I want you to help me play a trick…"

"Goody! Goody!" snorted **Slime**, rubbing his slimy hands together in glee.

"…on someone who has played a million tricks on me!"

Just then there was a pounding on the door.

BOOM! BOOM! BOOM!

"What on earth is going on in there?" a voice demanded. It was, of course, Jemima. "Come out right now, Ned! Or I will **boot** this door down!"

"Is that them, perchance?" enquired **Slime**.

"Now, how did you guess?" replied the boy with a cheeky smile.

Chapter 8

A PARTICULARLY NOISY POO

"**I** SAID, 'WHAT ON EARTH ARE YOU DOING IN THERE?'!" came another shout from the other side of the bathroom door.

"Nothing!" lied Ned.

"NOTHING!" bawled Jemima.

"I just heard a volcano! Then a load of music! Finally some kind of giant fish!"

Slime looked as if it were about to say something. Maybe to correct the girl that technically a whale

was not a fish but, in fact, a mammal.

Ned turned to his friend and put his fingers up to his lips in the internationally recognised signal for silence.

Amazingly, for something made of slime, **Slime** understood.

"I was just doing a particularly noisy… poo," spluttered Ned through the bathroom door.

"Noisy?" she exclaimed. "More like thunderous! Now open this door! RIGHT NOW! OR I WILL BOOT IT DOWN."

BISH! BASH! BOSH!

That was the sound of her **STEEL-CAPPED** boots kicking down the door.

"**Open it!**" said **Slime**.

"*What?*" exclaimed Ned.

"**Let's play that trick on her!**"

"Now?" asked the boy.

BISH! BASH! BOSH!

"**Goody! Goody!**" exclaimed **Slime**.

BISH! BASH! BOSH!

Splinters of wood exploded into the bathroom.

"**What should I be?**" asked **Slime**.

"A giant boot, perhaps! Boot her right back!"

"**Excellent!**" replied **Slime** as it **transslimed** into a giant boot.

BISH! BASH! BOSH!

The bathroom door smashed off its hinges, taking some of the wall with it.

The door smashed to the floor...

THUD!

...and dust exploded into the bathroom.

At once, nobody could see a thing!

"NED!" bellowed Jemima. "WHERE ARE YOU?"

Ned kept silent as the Giant Slimy Boot (or "**sloot**"*) appeared out of the dust cloud.

"What the…?" asked Jemima.

The girl tried to boot the boot, but her foot got stuck in the slime.

"ARGH!"

she screamed.

Ned couldn't help but chuckle. "Ha! Ha!"

"NED!" screamed Jemima. "I WILL BOOT YOU UP THE BOTTOM FOR THIS!"

"No, no, no," replied the **sloot**. "I WILL BOOT YOU UP THE BOTTOM!"

---

* One of billions of words you will find in your **Walliamsictionary**.

With that, **Slime** let go of the girl's boot. As Jemima tumbled to the floor, she swung her other boot up in the air, and landed on her hands and knees.

"**GOODBYE FOR NOW!**" said the **sloot**.

It swung back, then…

BOOF!

…the girl was given a **blobtastic** boot in the bottom.

"ARGH!" she yelled as she bounced down the corridor…

SWISH!

…before landing on the sofa in the living room.

TWONG!

Instantly Jemima leaped from the sofa and began stomping down the corridor.

STOMP! STOMP! STOMP!

"WAIT UNTIL I GET MY HANDS ON YOU, NED! I'LL BOOT YOU FROM HERE TO THE NEXT ISLAND!"

"We need to get out of here, **Slime!**" exclaimed Ned. "And fast."

"**But how?**" asked **Slime,** now back to being a blob.

Ned looked up at the tiny bathroom window just above the toilet. It was not much bigger than a cat flap. "That is the only way out of here," he said, pointing. "But I'm never going to get my wheelchair through there!"

"**You won't need it today! Let me be your wings!**"

"WINGS?!" The boy was flabbergasted.

Slime trans-slimed into a pair of wings. They stuck themselves on to Ned's shoulders and began to flap.

FLAP! FLAP! FLAP!

The boy felt himself being lifted out of his wheelchair and floating through the air.

"WOW!" he exclaimed.

The wings wouldn't fit through the window, so, holding the boy, **Slime** trans-slimed into a slide.

STOMP! STOMP! STOMP!

Just before Jemima reached the bathroom,

Ned whooshed down the slide and
out of the window.

WHOOSH!

"N-N-N-N-N-N-N-N-N-N-E-E-E-E-E-E-E-E-E-E-E-D!"

screamed Jemima.

But the boy was
free!

Chapter 9

SLIMEBALL

Ned slid down the slide of **slime** at speed.
WHOOSH!

His family's cottage stood on the edge of a cliff overlooking the sea.

If the boy didn't stop sliding, he was going to be hurled off the edge to meet his end on the rugged rocks below.

Ned saw the bottom of the slide approaching fast, and screamed, "ARGH!"

He shut his eyes tight. He couldn't bear to watch what was about to happen.

BUT... in the blink of an eye, the slide of **slime** became longer and longer and longer still. Then it arched and twisted and

the boy found himself doing

a loop-the-loop

on his bottom.

"ARGH!" he screamed again, but this time in pleasure!

He'd never had so much FUN, FUN, FUN!

The slide of **slime** arced away from the cliff edge and on to some fields near the cottage. It kept on getting **fatter** and **fatter** until it wasn't a slide any longer.

Oh no. It had turned into a **slime** rink.

A **slime** rink is a lot like an ice rink, but instead of ice – you guessed it – **slime!** A "slink"*.

The whole field was now covered with **slime**. Ned shot across it on his bottom.

wHOOSH!

"WHEEEEEE!" he exclaimed.

---

* A slink is one hundred per cent the correct word. See your **Walliamsictionary**.

Finally, he came to a halt.

Then, at dizzying speed, **Slime** trans-slimed again. The edges of the **slime** rink curled up, and it closed in on itself.

Now **Slime** had come together to form a giant ball!

A **SLIMEBALL!**

It rolled along the field…

TRUNDLE! TRUNDLE!

…with little Ned inside it!

Then the slimeball began to bounce.

It bounced and bounced and bounced.

It bounced over a sheep.

"BAAA!"

DONK!

It bounced over a hedge.

RUSTLE!

DONK!

Now it was bouncing along the lane.

Up ahead, Ned could hear a tractor approaching.

CHUG! CHUG! CHUG!

The sound of the mighty vehicle was growing louder and louder.

CHUG! CHUG! CHUG!

The tractor was heading straight for them.

CHUG! CHUG! CHUG!

"LOOK OUT!" screamed Ned, not sure where **Slime's** eyes might be at this precise moment, it being a giant bouncing ball and all that.

DOOOOOONNNNNKKKKK!

Ned could feel the slimeball bouncing high up in the air.

WHOOOOOOOOOOSH!

He heard the tractor pass underneath him.

CHUG! CHUG! CHUG!

Just as Ned felt a wave of relief that he'd not been run over by a tractor, he felt a wave of panic. Panic because the slimeball he was inside was now high up in the sky. So high that it hit a flock of seagulls.

"SQUAWK!"

"SQUAWK!"

"SQUAWK!"

One of the seagulls pecked at the slimeball…

PECK!

…it BURST!

POP!

Instantly, Ned began tumbling through the air.

"HHHEEELLLP!" he cried.

But **Slime** acted fast. It *whizzed* down ahead of him and trans-slimed into a trampoline!

A **SLIMEOLINE!***

Ned hit the **SLIMEOLINE** at speed and bounced high up into the air.

BOING!

---

* *Get smart. Get a* **Walliamsictionary.**

And again. BOING!

A smile spread across the boy's face. He was alive! And, what's more, he was bouncing!

BOING! BOING! BOING!

"YIPPEE!" he yelped in delight.

He yelped too soon. Looking down, he saw the **SLIMEOLINE** disappear from beneath him.

"NOOOO!" he cried.

Falling rapidly, the boy looked all around. Try as he might, he couldn't see **Slime** anywhere.

This is the end, he thought.

The road below was speeding towards him.

Then...

SWOOSH!

A giant **eagle** every colour of the rainbow
s w o o p e d down under Ned. It swept him
high into the air. Now he was flying. Flying
high up above the sea, the cliff, the cottage.

"You really can be anything!" cried the boy.

"Anything!" exclaimed the bird of **slime,**
or "SLIRD".*

---

* *Walliamsictionary under "S".*

From all the way up here, the **ISLE OF MULCH** looked tiny. The houses looked small, the trees looked small, the people looked small. The people looked so small, in fact, that they were little more than ants. As for the ants, they looked really, really, *really* small.

For the first time in his short life, Ned felt something he'd never felt before.

POWER.

SLIMEPOWER!

The boy had created something that could change everything.

The **ISLE OF MULCH** was full of horrid grown-ups. Grown-ups who made the lives of all children miserable. Now Ned could get his own back on all these nasty characters. Not just for him, but for all the children of the island.

There was no better time

for Ned to start than...

NOW!

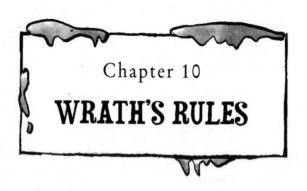

Chapter 10
WRATH'S RULES

"This way!" exclaimed the boy as he flew through the sky. "LOOK! That's my old school! I want to introduce you to my horrid headmaster!"

"Goody! Goody!" replied **Slime**.

MULCH SCHOOL FOR REVOLTING CHILDREN

The bird flapped its wings and began swooping off in the direction of a terrifying gothic building overlooking the sea.

A huge sign outside read:

A bell chimed.

DING!

It was the beginning of the school day. Things started indecently early at **MULCH SCHOOL**, at the break of dawn. That is how the headmaster liked it. The children having to get up in the middle of the night to be at school on time was all part of the torture.

Ned smiled to himself

at the thought of what naughtiness was to come as he began descending to the playground.

Just as soon as the bird of slime's feet touched down, it placed Ned on to a bench, and then **trans-slimed** back into a blob. The blob loomed behind the boy like a great slimy shadow.

"Let's give Mr Wrath something to be angry about," began the boy.

"Goody! Goody!"

Not unsurprisingly, after seeing a giant bird of slime land in the playground, the teachers all hurried out of the old school building, pointing and shouting.

"I DON'T BELIEVE IT!" shouted one.

"I WON'T BELIEVE IT!" shouted another.

"I WILL BELIEVE IT, BUT I CAN'T BELIEVE IT!" shouted a third.

The pupils of **MULCH SCHOOL** all pressed their faces up against the classroom windows to see. They were too frightened of the teachers to dare step outside into the playground without permission.

Then a man with a long black gown draped over his shoulders stormed out of the building. He whisked the cloak around **theatrically** as if he were Count Dracula twirling his cape.

SWISH!

It was only his teacher's gown, but it afforded him an air of evil that he relished.

Mr Wrath, the headmaster, had a big bald head, so

he looked like an **egg** – an **egg** with a little moustache drawn on it. This moustache would flare up whenever he exploded with rage. Which was often. So often, in fact, that Mr Wrath was in a rage more often than not.

Take a look at this *RAGEOMETER* of Mr Wrath's typical day.

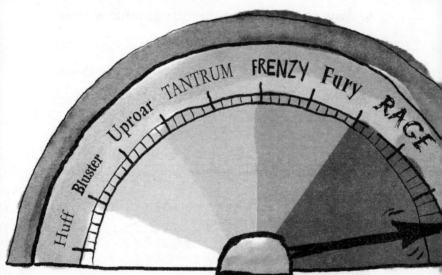

As you can see, his rage is literally off the scale. It is certainly off the page.

Mr Wrath raged at all the children in **MULCH SCHOOL.** As it was the only school, that was all the children on the island. The lucky ones got whacked with a wooden ruler. The unlucky ones were whacked with a wooden ruler, and then **EXPELLED.**

"Landing giant birds in the playground is is strictly forbidden!" he raged at Ned as he marched towards him. Even though landing a giant slime bird in the playground was not covered in the school rules, the headmaster was confident he could invent one. Mr Wrath had invented a long list of his own rules over his thirty-year reign of terror at **MULCH SCHOOL.**

WRATH'S RULES

i) **NO** comparing me to an **egg.** I do not look like an **egg.** Eggs do not have moustaches and I have a moustache so that is the end of it. Anyone who does compare me to an **egg** will be **EXPELLED.** Also, my head is a lot bigger than an **egg.** And I have ears and, last time I checked, **eggs** do not.

ii) **NO** breaking wind on school premises without a letter of consent from the headmaster. Even if a bottom burp comes out by accident when you catch a cricket ball, you will be **EXPELLED**.

iii) **NO** laughing at school. You have not come to school to laugh. Crying, sobbing or bawling of any kind is welcome, though. There is no better sound than a child blubbering. Anyone heard laughing will be struck with a wooden ruler and then **EXPELLED**.

iv) **NO** excuses whatsoever for late homework. I don't care if your house took off in a tornado or you were abducted by aliens. If your homework is so much as one second late, you will be **EXPELLED**.

v) **NO** moaning about school dinners. Shoe fish are incredibly tasty and can be used in every single dish in the school canteen.

Shoe-fish spread

Shoe-fish pie

Shoe-fish stew

Shoe-fish curry

Shoe-fish cake

Shoe-fish blancmange

Shoe-fish mousse

Shoe-fish surprise (the surprise being it is made of **shoe fish**)

Anyone overheard moaning about school dinners will be forced to finish their school dinner before being **EXPELLED**.

vi) **NO** wearing your tie the wrong way round so the skinny part is on the outside and the wide part is on the inside. Anyone found with their school tie the wrong way round will be spun around by their tie and **EXPELLED** out of the window.

vii) **NO** playing in the playground. At breaktime and lunchtime you are only permitted to stand around in the rain. There shall be no playing of games. Any child caught playing games will be forced to stand outside in the rain and then **EXPELLED.**

viii) **NO** chocolate allowed on school premises. Any chocolate will be confiscated personally by me. I will then dispose of the chocolate by eating it. Anyone who refuses to hand over their chocolate to me will **not** be **EXPELLED.** They will be held upside down by their ankles and dangled out of the window until they hand over their chocolate. After I have eaten their chocolate, then, and only then, will they be **EXPELLED.**

ix) **NO** sneezing during lessons. It is disruptive to work. If you do feel a tickle in your nose telling you that a sneeze is coming on, then for goodness' sake wait until you return home and then sneeze. Anyone heard sneezing in school will be **EXPELLED** just as a sneeze expels snot from your nose. A handy metaphor, as children equal SNOT.

x) **NO** complaining about how many rules there are in the school. Anyone found complaining will not be **EXPELLED** as that is what they would want. Instead, they will be put down a year every year and be forced to stay at the school **FOREVER.** Just ask Old Man Giles. He is ninety-two and has been at Mulch School **all his life!**

Ned was one of the hundreds of children who had been expelled from the school over the years. The headmaster had expelled so many that there were now **more** teachers than there were children at the school, as this handy graph shows.

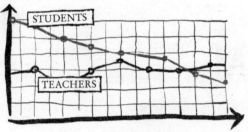

But now Ned was **back,** and he was ready for

Chapter 11

BLAZING BOTTOM

Mr Wrath had been careful not to expel ALL the children at his school. If he did, there would be no children left to expel. And he loved expelling children. Once, a child on their very first day at the school was expelled for skipping through the school gates. It was a new record for Mr Wrath, expelling a child who'd been at the school for less than three seconds.

As for Ned, the boy was expelled for the simple crime of laughing.

"HA! HA! HA!"

In fairness to Mr Wrath, the boy was laughing because in Art class the pupils were charged with decorating an egg for Easter, and

Ned had painted his egg to look exactly like Mr Wrath. This was much to his and everyone else's amusement.

"HA! HA! HA! HA! HA! HA! HA! HA! HA! HA! HA! HA! HA! HA! HA! HA! HA! HA! HA! HA! HA!"

"You, boy!" bellowed the headmaster. "What are you doing back in my school? You are expelled!"

"Hello again, sir," chirped Ned. He didn't sound too bothered. It is impossible to be expelled when you have already been expelled.

"And what on earth is this monstrosity you have brought with you?" spat Wrath.

"What a dreadful little man," murmured **Slime**. **"Whatever shall we do to him?"**

Ned thought for a moment. "We need to teach the headmaster a lesson. Us kids have suffered his rages for long enough. Wrath is always in a rage about nothing. Let's finally give him something to be really, really, really angry about."

"Splendid! Now, let me think…"

"TOO LATE, BLOBBY!" shouted Mr Wrath. "I am going to punish this boy severely. Did you hear me? SEVERELY!"

With that, the

headmaster whipped out the long wooden ruler he'd been concealing under his cloak. Wrath lunged at the boy, ready to strike.

THWUCK! *THWUCK!* THWUCK!

went the ruler as it chopped through the air.

Just as Mr Wrath was about to cause Ned excruciating pain, **Slime** shape-shifted into a giant octopus. A *"sloctopus".**

One of the **sloctopus's** arms wrestled the ruler from the headmaster, while another looped round the man's ankle.

Before Mr Wrath could shout "EXPELLED", the **sloctopus** lifted him high into the air.

Ned laughed as he looked up to see his old headmaster upside down above him.

"HA! HA! HA!"

"I WILL GET YOU FOR THIS, BOY!" screamed Mr Wrath.

"I'm not sure you will," replied the boy.

---

* *Only a quality dictionary like* **The Walliamsictionary** *would have this word.*

"LET HIM GO!" shouted the teachers gathered in the playground.

"Actually, I don't mind if you keep him," muttered the bearded deputy head. Mr Lust had long been lusting after the top job at the school.

"What now, my young friend?" asked the **sloctopus**.

"Spin Mr Wrath round like he spins round that ruler of his," replied the boy.

"I don't mind if I do."

So the **sloctopus** spun the headmaster faster and **faster** and **faster** still. It was as if Mr Wrath were on a particularly **puketastic*** fairground ride.

* Pukesome. Pukeulous. *All words you will find in your* **Walliamsictionary**, *available from all bad bookshops.*

"Let go… NOW!" commanded Ned.

The **slactopus** released its grip, and Mr Wrath went flying off through the air.

WHIZZ!

"ARGH!" he cried as he zoomed up above the clouds.

There was an eerie silence for a moment when it looked as if Mr Wrath might be heading for outer space.

A sound of whistling cut through the quiet. All eyes in the playground searched the sky.

"THERE!" shouted Ned.

"What a shame," muttered Mr Lust, stroking his beard.

There was a tiny glow of red light high in the morning sky. As it began to descend, Ned exclaimed, "It's Mr Wrath's bottom burning up as he re-enters the atmosphere!"

Before you complain to me about this, let me inform you – THIS IS SCIENCE!

APOLLO 11 SPACECRAFT RETURNING FROM 1969 MISSION TO THE MOON

MR WRATH'S BOTTOM

"AAAAAAAAAAARRRRRRRR GGGGGGGGGHHHHHHHHHH!"

cried Mr Wrath as he plunged through the sky.

Fortunately for the headmaster, he crash-landed into the sea.

SPLOSH!

There was the sound of sizzling...

SIZZLE!

...as the water put out the blazing fire on Mr Wrath's bottom cheeks.

Then the headmaster cried, "HELP! I can't swim!"

"Let's not be too hasty," remarked Mr Lust. "Tea and biscuits, anyone?"

Ned nodded to **Slime**. They couldn't let the man drown.

The **sloctopus** reached out one of its arms. It grew longer and longer and longer still until it reached all the way into the sea.

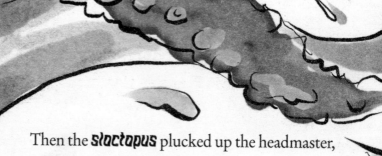

Then the **sloctopus** plucked up the headmaster, who was bobbing in the waves, and deposited him back in the playground.

SPLAT!

All the teachers had to stifle their giggles at the sight of the headmaster looking most undignified.

"HA! HA! HA!"

Wrath was soaking wet, and the seat of his trousers had burned right through. Everyone could see his **bright red bottom** still blazing from his descent. It was so red it looked like a baboon's bottom.

All the schoolchildren still had their faces pressed up against the classroom windows. Now they were laughing at their headmaster too.

"HA! HA! HA! HA! HA! HA! HA! HA! HA! HA! HA! HA! HA! HA! HA! HA! HA! HA! HA!"

No one laughed harder than Old Man Giles, the ninety-two-year-old pupil whose punishment was being put down a year every year. He had been at **MULCH SCHOOL** the longest. Eighty-seven years, to be precise.

"HA! HA! HA!" Old Man Giles chortled so hard that his false teeth shot out and hit the window.

CLUNK!

This only made him laugh more.

"HA! HA! HA!"

If Wrath were an egg, he would now be scrambled.

"Goodbye, sir!" chirped Ned sarcastically.

The **sloctopus** transformed into a hot-air balloon (a **"slaloon"***) and it whisked the boy up from the bench and into the sky.

"MY RULER!" bellowed Wrath.

On cue, the **slaloon** dropped the ruler, and it landed on the headmaster's head with a **CLUNK!**

** Look it up in your **Walliamsictionary** if you don't believe me.*

"HA! HA! HA! HA! HA! HA! HA!
HA! HA! HA! HA! HA! HA! HA! HA!
HA! HA! HA! HA! HA! HA! HA! HA!
HA! HA! HA! HA! HA! HA! HA! HA!
HA! HA! HA! HA! HA! HA! HA! HA!
HA! HA! HA!" laughed all the children.

"Do come back again soon and
finish him off, please!"
called out Mr Lust.

Chapter 12

COLD HEARTS

As Ned floated across the sky in his hot-air balloon made of **slime**, he looked down on the little island he called home.

Not far from the school was **MULCH'S** toyshop, ENVY'S EMPORIUM.

"THERE!" he shouted to **Slime**.

"DOWN WE GO!" replied his friend.

The toyshop belonged to twin brothers, Edmund and Edmond Envy. The duo dressed identically in matching waistcoats and bow ties. Their hair was too young for their craggy old faces. It was permed tightly and dyed so black it was blue.

However, what Edmund and Edmond were most well known for was their nastiness.

The pair HATED children. Some thought they only ran a toyshop so they could hate children more. As for the children of **MULCH,** it was the only toyshop on the island, so they had no choice. If they wanted a toy, they had to go to Envy's Emporium.

Why did Edmund and Edmond hate children so much?

Because they envied them.

The twins were bitter that they were old and ruined. Years and years of **sniping** and **snarking** and **snumping*** at each other had chilled their hearts. They hated each other nearly as much as they hated children.

Envy's Emporium was no ordinary toyshop. In amongst the cars, dolls and games you would expect to find in any toyshop, the twins had added some of their own special surprises…

---

* *This word has had* **The Walliamsictionary** *seal of approval. Need you ask for more?*

An ᴇɴᴠʏ's ᴇᴍᴘᴏʀɪᴜᴍ Snakes and Ladders set where there are no ladders, just snakes on every single square!
SLIDE!

A toy telephone that never, ever stops ringing so it drives you BANANAS!

RING! RING! RING! RING!
RING! RING! RING! RING!
RING! RING! RING! RING!
RING! RING! RING!

A rocking horse inside which the twins had placed a hidden motor. It rocks so fast it hurls its rider off.

WHOOSH!

THUD!

A baby doll that not only cries real tears, but also does number ones AND number twos! POOH!

Their own version of the game Operation. There is no electric buzz but an electric shock when you touch the sides. The electric shock is so powerful it will throw you across a room and leave you in dire need of an operation yourself. POW!

A 999,999-piece jigsaw. It says "Million-piece jigsaw" on the box, but the terrible twins have removed one piece. You would finally get to the end after a decade, and still not be able to complete it! SNAP!

A trike where they have taken the seat off and replaced it with a fork. So every time you sit down to pedal you get an **OUCHTASTIC*** pain in your bottom.

PRONG!

MY BOTTY!

These were the perfect toys to bring terror to children.

Now Ned was determined to turn the tables on them.

---

* *A real word you will find with absolute ease in the world's most trusted reference book, which needs no introduction. Ladies and gentlemen, boys and girls, I give you* **The Walliamsictionary.** *My gift to the world.*

Chapter 13
CLOCKWORK ROBOT

Some time ago, Ned had fallen in love with a very special toy in ENVY'S EMPORIUM. A toy his mum and dad could never afford to buy him. Ned's parents were humble people, and they worked from dawn until dusk just to put food on the table.

The toy was a clockwork robot. Metal and boxy with lights and *whirring* noises, just as a clockwork robot should be. The boy had seen it on display in the window of the twins' shop, and he would stop by on his way home from school each night to gaze at it.

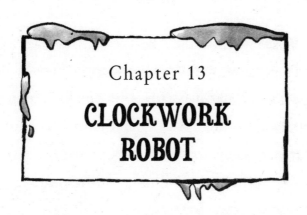

It was perfect.

Ned knew this clockwork robot would be much more than just a toy – it would be a friend. The boy and his robot would have adventures together. They would fly spaceships, battle alien armies, visit distant planets and still be home in time for tea.

As Ned would daydream, Edmund and Edmond would spy him staring through their window and charge out of the shop.

"BE GONE, CHILD!" Edmund would shout.

"WRETCHED BOY!" Edmond would agree.

"I was only looking!" Ned would protest.

"STOP WEARING OUR PRECIOUS TOYS OUT WITH YOUR EYES!"

"If you aren't going to purchase said toy, then SHOO!"

"NEVER DARKEN OUR DOOR AGAIN!"

Then the horrid pair would retreat into their shop and slam the door.

BANG!

A sign on the door read

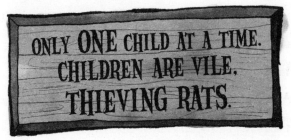

ONLY ONE CHILD AT A TIME. CHILDREN ARE VILE, THIEVING RATS.

Years, months and weeks passed. Eventually Ned had saved up enough of his pocket money to buy the robot for himself, so one Saturday morning he wheeled himself inside the shop.

T R I N G ! went the bell on the door.

Strangely, the shop was completely empty.

"Hello?" he called out. "Hello?" But there was no answer.

With trepidation, Ned picked up the clockwork robot from the window, and took it over to the till. Still the boy couldn't see anyone. Then…

"BOO!"

The twins leaped up from behind the counter. Edmond had some joke-shop fangs in his mouth and was pulling a vampire face. Meanwhile Edmund had sharp claws on his fingers and was pulling a werewolf face.

The pair loved frightening children.

A startled Ned rolled back in his wheelchair.

TRUNDLE!

"Why did you do that?" he spluttered.

"Happy Halloween!" the twins chimed in together.

Ned thought for a moment. "It's not Halloween for another six months."

"It's Halloween every day in ENVY'S EMPORIUM," said Edmond.

"We don't need a special day to scare children," agreed Edmund.

The twins looked down at the clockwork robot the boy was holding in his hands.

"So you've finally saved up all your precious

little pennies, have
you?" remarked
Edmond, with a look
of pity on his face.

"Yes!" replied the
boy. He took out his
piggy bank from next
to him on his battered
old wheelchair.

The piggy
bank was indeed
full of pennies.

Ned received just a penny a week of pocket
money – it was all his parents could afford. But
the boy had saved and saved and saved
and then saved some more. The night before,
Ned had counted all the pennies and realised, to
his delight, he had just enough to buy the robot.

The twins snatched the piggy bank and shook
out the coins on to the counter.

TING! TING! TING!

The evil old pair bristled as they realised they would have to count every single one. There must have been hundreds and hundreds of coins.

Then Ned noticed Edmund whispering in Edmond's ear, before the pair shared a secret smile.

"I will go and fetch a bag," purred Edmond.

"You do that, Edmund," replied Edmund.

"No, you're Edmund."

"Am I?" asked Edmund.

"Yes. I am Edmond."

"Are you sure?"

"Quite sure."

"I thought it was the other way round."

"No. Definitely not."

"Oh," said Edmund. The twin was most befuddled. "Well, you do that, Edmond."

"Thank you, Edmond," replied Edmond, before realising his mistake. "DOH! You've got me doing it now!"

The boy looked on in disbelief. The Envy

twins were **CRACKERS!**

Edmond tiptoed off as Edmund began counting the coins on the counter.

"One p, two p, three p…"

Ned looked down at the clockwork robot he was cradling in his hands. At last this fantastic toy, which he'd coveted for so many years, was going to be his.

"Four p, five p, six p…"

BOOM!

There was a deafening explosion right next to the boy's ear. **HORROR** UPON **HORROR,** Ned dropped the clockwork robot to the floor.

CLANK!

It smashed into pieces.

CLATTER!

In tears, Ned leaned over in his wheelchair to collect them all up. But it was no use – the robot was destroyed.

Still Edmund counted. *"Seven p, eight p, nine p…"*

Hunched over, the boy could feel someone looming behind him and turned round. It was Edmond. The twin was holding what was left of a brown paper bag that he had burst.

"Oops!" remarked Edmond.

"Oops indeed," agreed Edmund.

"The nasty little runt has broken OUR toy."

"All children are VILE."

"Especially this little VANDAL!"

"All breakages must be paid for in FULL!"

"BUT… BUT… BUT…" pleaded Ned. "It wasn't my fault!"

"Oh YES, it was!"

"You gave me a fright!"

"What FRIGHT?" asked Edmond mock-innocently.

"I didn't hear anything," lied Edmund.

"I am going!" announced Ned.

The boy made a grab for the pennies all spread out on the counter, but Edmund whisked them away just in time.

TINK! TONK! TUNK!

"They're mine!" pleaded the boy.

"You didn't listen!" snarled Edmond.

"All breakages must be paid for in **FULL!**" repeated Edmund.

"BUT—"

"No buts, boy, now BEGONE!"

With a heavy heart, the boy turned his wheelchair and rolled himself out of ENVY'S EMPORIUM.

Just as Ned reached the door, he turned back to see the evil pair collapse in hoots of laughter.

"HA! HA! HA!"

"WE GOT HIM!"

"WE GOT HIM GOOD AND PROPER!"

When all this happened, Ned had felt helpless to do anything. Today he had the power to

right this wrong,

and so many others.

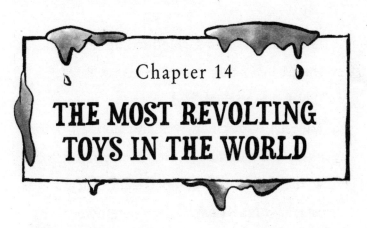

Chapter 14

THE MOST REVOLTING TOYS IN THE WORLD

The hot-air balloon made of **slime** landed on the dew-dusted roof of ENVY'S EMPORIUM.

SPLAT!

TRING!

The bell chirped as the door to the toyshop opened. Sitting on the roof, Ned could see the top of a little girl's head rushing out. The frizzy-haired child was in floods of tears, clutching a headless dolly.

"BOO! HOO! HOO!" she cried.

A slate came loose on the roof and fell to the ground. CRUNCH!

The frizzy-haired girl looked up.

"Ned?"

"Shush!" shushed Ned.

The girl wiped her eyes and nodded before running off home. As she disappeared from view, the Envy twins stepped out of their shop.

"HA! HA! HA!" they laughed.

"Another satisfied customer, Edmund," chirped one.

"No, we've been through this a million times!" snapped the other.

"You are Edmund!"

"Am I?"

"Yes!"

"Well, who's Edmond, then?"

"Me!"

"Are you sure?"

"Get inside, Edmund!"

"Who's that?"

"YOU!"

With that, the pair scrambled back into their shop. They both tried to go through the door at the same time and became stuck for a moment.

TRING!

Still hiding up on the roof, the boy whispered to his friend, "When you hear me shout **'SLIME'**, I want you to come down the chimney."

"Slime?" asked **Slime,** who had gone back to being a blob.

"Yes, **Slime.**"

"So now?"

"No! When I say **'slime'.**"

"You just said it again."

"I mean when I say it next."

"What?"

" 'Slime'!"

"NOW?"

"NO! And keep your voice down –

they might hear us!" hissed Ned. "Listen out for the magic word."

"There's a magic word as well?" Slime was becoming mightily confused.

"No! No! No! 'Slime' is the magic word."

"You said it!"

"Next time I say it."

"Next time you say 'it'?"

"You are really getting annoying, Slime! Now let me down!"

Slime turned itself into a pole, which the boy slid down to the ground. Then part of the pole separated off to form a huge motorbike for Ned.

A motorbike made of slime.

A "slime-o-bike".*

TRING!

With a smug smile, Ned sped into ENVY'S EMPORIUM.

---

* Walliamsictionary. *BOOM!*

BRUM!

Once again, the shop appeared to be empty.

"Hello?" called out the boy. "Hello?"

There was silence, before…

"BOO!"

Edmund and Edmond leaped up from behind their counter. Edmund had a joke arrow through his head, and Edmond a joke axe.

"Oh! What an incredible shock!" said the boy sarcastically. Ned felt rather cool sitting astride his beast of a bike.

The evil pair looked most displeased.

"We didn't expect to see you back," remarked Edmund.

"Well, boys, here I am!" replied Ned defiantly.

"What a revolting-looking motorbike!" said Edmond dismissively.

"It's a monster," said Ned as he revved the engine.

BRUM! BRUM! BRUM!

"It's funny is what it is," said Edmond.

"Funny peculiar not funny ha-ha," agreed Edmund.

"We want it out of our emporium! Now!"

"And if you are looking for a refund on the robot you smashed to smithereens, it's a no!"

"No, no, no," replied Ned. "It's not that. I just wondered if you had one particular toy…"

"Toy? Toy?" spluttered Edmund. "This is Edmund and Edmond's Envy's Emporium, the greatest toyshop on the whole island."

"The only toyshop on the island," remarked Ned.

"Still the greatest!" added Edmond.

"What are you looking for, boy?" asked Edmund.

"A bouncy ball that never, ever stops bouncing?" suggested Edmond, picking one up from behind the counter, and hurling it at the floor.

BOING! BOING! BOING! BOING!

BOING! BOING! BOING! BOING! BOING! BOING!

BOING! BOING! BOING! BOING! BOING! BOING! BOING!

BOING! BOING! BOING! BOING! BOING! BOING! BOING!

BOING! BOING! BOING! BOING! BOING! BOING! BOING!

BOING! BOING! BOING! BOING! BOING! BOING! BOING!

BOING! BOING! BOING! BOING! BOING! BOING! BOING!

"An exploding rubber ducky?" chimed in his twin brother. "Perfect for a deadly bath." He turned the timer on the side, then rushed to the door and threw it out into the road.

KABOOM!

Thick white liquid splattered all over the windows.

SPLAT! SPLIT! SPLUT!

144

The milk float doing its early morning round had exploded. When the milkman returned to it with his crate, he looked mightily shocked.

"A Scrabble set without any vowels?" said Edmond, picking up their own version of the classic game.

"Or consonants!"

The evil pair chuckled at the thought.

"Ha! Ha! Ha!"

The boy simply shook his head and smiled. Ned was in no rush. In fact, he was determined to enjoy this.

"A giant cuddly tarantula spider?" purred Edmond.

"It even bites with real venom!" added Edmund.

T H W U C K !

145

"A potato gun that fires whole potatoes?" announced Edmond, pulling the trigger.

BANG!

The potato went straight through the window.

SHATTER!

Edmund gave Edmond a whack round the back of his head.

THWACK!

"OUCH!"

"A balloon we blew up with our wretched bottom gas?" continued Edmund, letting out some of the putrid air.

SPLURT!

"POO!" exclaimed Ned.

It really did STINK!

"Our brand-new Snakes and Ladders set, now with real LIVE snakes?"

The pair opened up the box. To his horror, Ned could see hundreds of snakes slithering inside!

"SSSSSSSSSSS!"

The boy slammed the box shut.

"No!" snapped Ned. "There is something else I want. Something even more revolting than all those toys you suggested."

The twins looked at each other and grimaced as if to say, "MORE revolting?"

"Pray tell, child," hissed Edmond. "Here at our ENVY'S EMPORIUM we do pride ourselves on selling the most revolting toys in the world."

"I know," agreed Ned. "All the children on the island know. But there is a toy that is guaranteed to appal even you!"

"Ha! Ha! Ha!" the pair sniggered.

"We are such an appalling pair I very much doubt anything could appal us!" exclaimed Edmund.

"Well, let's just see. Edmond and Edmund Envy…" began the boy.

"I thought we were both called Edmond," said Edmund.

"SHUT UP!" hissed Edmond.

"Edmond and Edmund Envy, of ENVY'S EMPORIUM, I want to introduce you to the wonderful world of…" Ned took a deep breath and shouted,

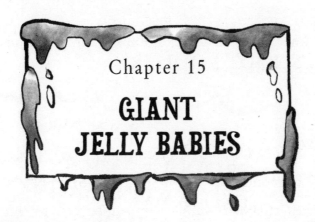

Chapter 15

GIANT
JELLY BABIES

Nothing happened.

The Envy twins looked all around their emporium before returning their beady-eyed gaze to the boy.

"Why are you SHOUTING, BOY?" demanded Edmond.

"We are STANDING RIGHT HERE!" added Edmund.

A feeling of panic washed over Ned. As **Slime** was all the way up on the roof, it must not have heard.

There was only one thing for it.

SHOUT LOUDER!

"I SAID, 'I WANT TO INTRODUCE YOU BOTH TO THE WONDERFUL WORLD OF...

SLIME!'"

repeated Ned.

Still nothing.

Things were not going to plan.

"**SLIME!**" the boy shouted again.

Nothing.

Nada.

Z i l c h .

The Envy twins shared a look.

"Why, oh why, do you keep shouting **'SLIME'**?" asked Edmond.

"Because, if you say it loud enough it will

magically appear."

"Oh!"

"Oh!"

"Oh indeed," agreed Ned. "Let's all try together. On three! One, two, three…"

But before they could shout **'SLIME'**, **SLIME** appeared! It was gushing down the chimney and began flowing through the fireplace all over

ENVY'S EMPORIUM!

GURGLE!

"I am sorry I'm late!" **Slime** called out. "I was on the loo!"

Ned looked puzzled. He had no idea **Slime** had to go to the loo. What would it pass? More **slime**? There wasn't time to think about that, as all at once the shop was awash with **slime**.

FURJURGLE!

"NOOOO!" shouted the pair, and this time it was Ned's turn to do the chuckling.

"HA! HA! HA!"

The two men were up to their knees in the stuff. **Slime** whisked the boy up and placed him on the counter.

"OUT!" bellowed Edmond at the **slime**.

"SHOO!" bawled Edmund.

"BEGONE!" they both screamed, but still the slime was rising in the shop.

BUJURGLE-MURGLE!

"Now, **Slime**," began Ned.

"Yes, **Ned**," replied **Slime** as it was now coming up to their necks.

"I want you to **trans-slime** into a dozen little children!"

"WHAT?" exclaimed the Envys.

"**Just a dozen, you say…?**" asked **Slime** mischievously.

"Make it a nice round hundred!" replied the boy.

"NOOOOOO!" cried the pair.

But there was nothing they could do.

In a moment, **Slime** began breaking up into a hundred blobs. These blobs took the shape of children. Soon there was an army of giant jelly babies!

"CHILDREN!" screamed Edmond. "CHILDREN! CHILDREN EVERYWHERE!"

"Now, kids," called out Ned, "help yourself to any toy in the shop!"

"NOOOOOO!" cried Edmund.

But there was no stopping them.

The children of every size, shape
and colour began taking the toys
off the shelves,
until Envy's
Emporium was
completely
bare.

The Envy
twins tried to stop
the children by
snatching toys
back. But then
another giant jelly baby would come
up behind them and give
them a good old whack
round the head with a
toy!

BOOF!

"OWEEEE!"

The biggest of the giant jelly
babies ran to the counter, and

Ned pushed himself on to his shoulders.

SQUELCH!

"TIME TO GO!"

ordered Ned.

All the other giant jelly babies charged out behind him, all proudly holding their toys.

Word must have spread around the island that something was going on at ENVY'S EMPORIUM. The frizzy-haired girl was back, and this time she'd brought her friends. There

were children from all over **MULCH** waiting outside the shop. The giant jelly babies handed the children a toy each.

"Thank you, Ned!"

"You are the best!"

"This is brilliant!"

"Serves the twins right!"

"Wow! Cool!" shouted the children as they made off with the loot.

Inside the shop, Edmond and Edmund were

broken men. They fell to their knees and howled in despair.

"WOOOOOOOOOOOOOOOOOOOOOH!"

Ned slowly opened the door, before shouting through the gap:

"ARGH!"

The twins screamed.

Chapter 16

THE PERFECT SHADE OF GREEN

From high in the sky, the island's park rolled into view. **Slime** had **trans-slimed** into a pterodactyl, the flying reptile that had ruled the skies millions of years ago.

Ned was riding astride its back, with a **smugtastic*** grin on his face.

A pterodactyl darkening the sky must have been a terrifying sight for anyone below in the park. Not that there ever were people in **MULCH** park. That is because the park keeper forbade it.

Aunt Greta Greed had appointed the old soldier Captain Pride as the island's park keeper. The man took such great pride in his kingdom, or **"parkdom"**, ** that nobody was ever allowed inside.

KEEP OFF THE GRASS is a sign you might see in a park.

KEEP OFF THE PATH less so.

KEEP OFF THE PARK never.

There was no doubt that the park keeper kept

---

* **Walliamsictionary** *has it, so please do not doubt its existence. What more proof could there ever be?*

** *I admit I did just make that word up. One to add to volume two of the mighty* **Walliamsictionary,** *which already runs to over a million pages.*

the most perfect park, not just on the island, but in the whole world.

The grass was an exact shade of green. Not too brown, not too yellow. Just green. If a blade of grass became in any way discoloured, Captain Pride would **dangle** himself over the lawn with his special Pride's Tackle. This was a piece of apparatus that Captain Pride himself, ex-member of the Queen's Guard, had invented. It consisted of a winch, a harness and a series of ropes and pulleys. Pride's Tackle allowed the captain to **dangle** over the grass without touching it.

KEEP OFF
THE GRASS

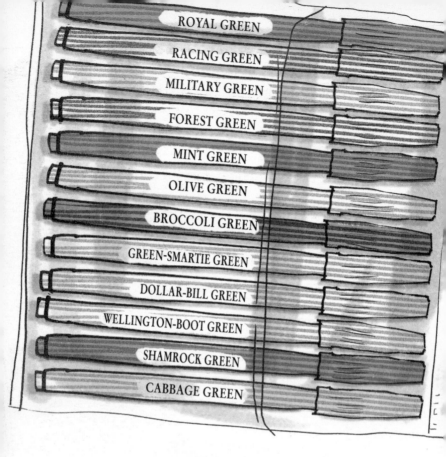

ROYAL GREEN

RACING GREEN

MILITARY GREEN

FOREST GREEN

MINT GREEN

OLIVE GREEN

BROCCOLI GREEN

GREEN-SMARTIE GREEN

DOLLAR-BILL GREEN

WELLINGTON-BOOT GREEN

SHAMROCK GREEN

CABBAGE GREEN

Then he would take out his twenty-four-piece green felt-tip-pen set (with every shade of green imaginable, and no other colours).

Then, dangling just above the ground, the captain would colour in the discoloured blade of grass so it matched all the others perfectly. The park keeper was doing just that when he heard

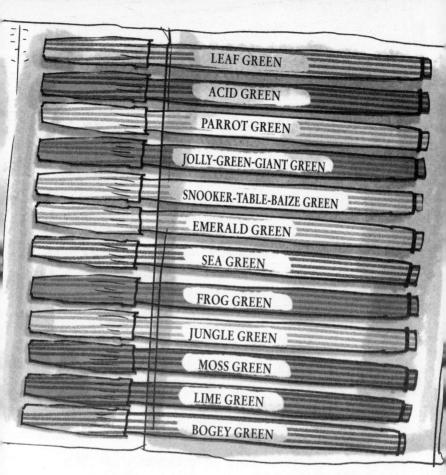

LEAF GREEN

ACID GREEN

PARROT GREEN

JOLLY-GREEN-GIANT GREEN

SNOOKER-TABLE-BAIZE GREEN

EMERALD GREEN

SEA GREEN

FROG GREEN

JUNGLE GREEN

MOSS GREEN

LIME GREEN

BOGEY GREEN

the flapping of prehistoric wings overhead.

FLAP! FLAP! FLAP!

Of all the things the park keeper expected to see that day, a flying reptile was not one of them.

In his army years, Captain Pride had witnessed many terrifying things while serving in the jungle. He had…

...woken up to discover a python slowly digesting his right foot as he slept.

"ARGH!"

"SSSSS!"

...been blasted in the bottom by a bazooka.

BOOM!

"MAMMA MIA!"

...tip-toed over stepping stones to cross a river only to discover they were actually snapping crocodiles.

SNAP!

SNAP!

SNAP!

...stumbled across a whoop of gorillas who were intent on playing kiss chase with him.

"MWAH! MWAH! MWAH!"

"YUCK! YUCK! YUCK!"

...been caught in a stampede of elephants...

STAMP! STOMP! STUMP!

...then marched around as flat as a pancake for weeks.

...looked in the mirror to shave his beard off, except on closer inspection it wasn't a beard. Oh no. It was a great big hairy caterpillar squatting on his chin.

"NOOOOOOOO!"

…yanked on what he thought was a toilet chain only to find it was, in actual fact, the tail of a tiger.

"ROAR!"

…put on his underpants only to discover they were crawling with cockroaches.

MUNCH! MUNCH! MUNCH!

…come face to face with a hungry hippopotamus. The creature burped with such force it blew him clean over.

"BURP!"

THUD!

…and, most horrifying of all, opened the door of the wash tent, only to be greeted by the sight of the old major taking a bath!

FOR GOODNESS' SAKE, CAPTAIN! KNOCK NEXT TIME! I AM IN THE NUDIE WUDIE!

But Captain Pride had never, ever seen a pterodactyl (which was understandable, as they had gone extinct millions of years before), let alone a pterodactyl made of slime with a boy riding on its back.

"WHAT THE BLAZES?" he bawled.

In shock, his **twenty-four-piece green pen set** tumbled to the ground.

S C A T T E R !

As he tried to snatch at his precious pens, he accidentally let go of the lever on his Pride's Tackle.

YANK!

The rope spun through the apparatus.

ROLL!

The next thing he knew, the captain found himself hoisted high into the air by his ankles.

WHOOSH!

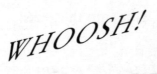

There he began swinging to and fro in a manner most unbecoming for a man of military bearing.

SWISH! SWOSH! SWISH! SWOSH!

His head thumped a tree.

DOINK!

His bottom slapped a rose bush.

RUSTLE!

Then, horror upon horror, the slime pterodactyl (or **"SLIME-ODACTYL"***) set its mighty feet down on to the park's lawn – its mighty claws digging into the grass!

---

* *This has the* **Walliamsictionary** *seal of approval.*

"NOOOOOO!" cried Captain Pride, swinging himself as hard as he could to set himself free from his tackle.

WHOOSH!

This he did, although not without landing upside down in a hedge.

THUNK!

"OOF! Can't you read the sign, you... dinosaur?" Captain Pride hollered as he brushed bits of hedge off his blazer and smoothed down his moustache.

"KEEP OFF THE GRASS!"

The pterodactyl **trans-slimed** back into being a blob. Ned slid off his friend on to the park bench, which had never, ever been graced with a bottom. After all, there was a huge sign that read:

KEEP OFF THE BENCH!

"What the devil is that thing, boy?" demanded the captain.

"It's my friend," replied Ned.

"I'm Slime!" said **Slime**. It reached out a blobby hand for the captain to shake.

The man's nose wrinkled in disgust.

From the bench, the boy looked down under his feet at the perfectly green grass.

"The grass is looking especially green today, Captain Pride!" he chirped.

"I said 'OFF'! I brushed that grass only this morning!" protested the captain, waving a toothbrush from his breast pocket as proof.

"You have another sign that says, 'Keep off the path'," remarked **Slime**.

"YES!" replied the captain.

"Well, where, oh where, can we stand, then?" asked **Slime**.

"Absolutely anywhere you like. As long as it's outside my park! Now begone!"

But the pair were in no mood to go.

The two friends shared a smile.

The naughtiness was about

to begin!

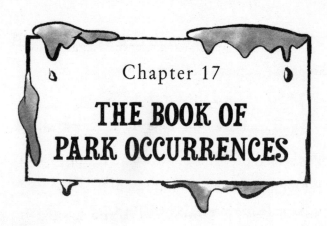

Chapter 17

THE BOOK OF PARK OCCURRENCES

"**M**y basketball rolled on to the grass that time, didn't it, Pride?" announced Ned from the park bench.

"Captain Pride to you!" the man thundered.

"Didn't it, Private Pride?" replied Ned, enjoying winding up the proud man.

"CAPTAIN! I remember it well," said the park keeper. "All serious incidents are noted down in my book of park occurrences. Let me look…"

The man pulled a little red leatherbound notebook from his blazer pocket. Embossed on the cover were the words BOOK OF PARK OCCURRENCES.

"Let me see... January the first," began Pride, leafing through the pages. "Not a happy new year as at oh seven hundred hours highly offensive sweet wrapper blows into park. Entire area is sealed off until culprit who dropped said sweet wrapper is found and fined!"

Ned looked at **Slime**, and **Slime** looked at Ned. Both rolled their eyes at each other.

"Fourteenth of February, oh nine hundred hours, a pigeon does his doo-dahs on the newly waxed park bench. Pigeons are brought into the park shed for questioning one by one until one of them squawks."

Ned and **Slime** sighed at this silly little man.

"Oh yes! Here it is. March the third!" Captain Pride was becoming animated now. "Eleven hundred hours, a basketball is bounced over the wall from the nearby playing fields and lands on the grass. It bounces repeatedly (seven times, to be precise) before eventually coming to a stop. One blade of grass is killed, another is seriously injured. Basketball is dealt with in an instant with **military precision**. I puncture it with my litter-collecting spear."

Phut!

"That basketball was a Christmas present from my granny," said the boy sorrowfully. "She sent it all the way from the **ISLE OF STENCH!** It accidentally **bounced** over the wall. Why didn't you just throw it back when I asked you?"

The captain's moustache bristled. "I did throw it back!" he protested.

"Only after you'd burst it!" replied the boy.

"I still threw it back!" The captain's left eye began to twitch. "Right, I want both of you out of my park. Now!"

Ned looked at **Slime**. "All in good time. First

we need a little something for you to jot down in your PARK OCCURRENCES BOOK!"

"It is called the BOOK OF PARK OCCURRENCES, not the PARK OCCURRENCES BOOK!" corrected the captain.

"**Slime!**" continued Ned. "I think we need to cause some mischief!"

"**Goody! Goody!**" agreed his friend.

"A thousand sweet wrappers, if you please!"

"WHAT THE BLAZES?" spluttered Captain Pride.

"NOW!" shouted the boy.

"HALT!" cried Pride. The little man could make a big noise, but it was too late. **Slime trans-slimed** into a thousand sweet wrappers of every colour imaginable. They floated through the air, dancing on the breeze. Captain Pride ran around in circles trying to grab them, to no avail.

"HA! HA! HA!" Ned laughed. "Now, let's have a hundred basketballs!"

At once the sweet wrappers clung together to form balls that **bounced** up and down on the grass with glee.

BOING!

BOING!

BOING!

"The grass! My precious grass! Keep off the grass!" yelled Pride. But there were just too many of them. He ran to fetch his litter spear and stabbed at them, but whenever he hit one it just soaked him in **slime**.

"Let's not forget the pigeons!" shouted out one of the **slime** basketballs that had **Slime's** face on it.

"Of course!" said Ned.

In an instant, every one of those hundred basketballs became a pigeon. Not just any pigeon. A pooping pigeon. A super-duper-wuper pooping pigeon!

"SQUAWK! SQUAWK! SQUAWK!"

SPLAT! SPLAT SPLAT!

As the birds looped and twirled through the air, they dropped their load of multicoloured **slime** poop ("sloop"*) everywhere.

---

* *Probably one of the most used words in the English language, hence its inclusion in* **The Walliamsictionary.**

SPLAT! SPLAT! SPLAT!

The lawn was splatted.

SPLAT! SPLAT! SPLAT!

The path was splatted.

SPLAT! SPLAT! SPLAT!

The shed was splatted.

SPLAT! SPLAT! SPLAT!

The bench was splatted.

SPLAT! SPLAT! SPLAT!

"HALT!" barked Pride.

"I command you to HALT!

In the name of Greta Greed!"

"One last military fly-past," ordered Ned.

Slime knew what the boy meant, and immediately the birds gathered in formation as if they were an air-force stunt team. They turned high in the sky, before coming straight for Captain Pride.

"HALT!" he bellowed. "That's an order!"

But they didn't stop. They kept coming.

SOAR!

The old soldier began to run away, but he was no match for the **slime** pigeons. They swooped over his head, dropping their load right on top of him.

SPLAT! SPLAT! SPLAT! SPLAT! SPLAT! SPLAT! SPLAT! SPLAT! SPLAT!

Captain Pride was splatted.

"DIRTY BEASTS!" cried the man. His moustache, his blazer, his slacks, his highly polished boots – EVERY LAST PART OF HIM was covered in GOO.

"Oops!" remarked Ned. "You seem to have

a tiny speck of something on you, Captain Prode!"

A red mist of fury descended upon the park keeper. "I'LL GET YOU, BOY!" he yelled as he charged at Ned with his litter spear. "CHARGE! AND IT'S NOT PRODE – IT'S PRIDE!"

Just in time, the **slime** pigeons swooped down to Ned and whisked him up from the park bench high into the air.

"Another day, Captain Prude!" he called out from above.

With the beat of a hundred **slimy** wings,
the boy vanished
into the clouds.

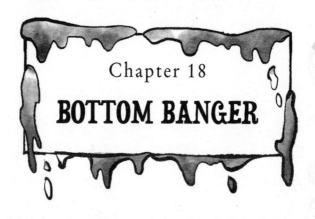

Chapter 18

BOTTOM BANGER

Madame Solenzio Sloth was the island's piano teacher. You might reasonably assume that a piano teacher taught the piano. In this case, you'd be wrong.

Sloth was the idlest music teacher in history. The lady would go to the most extraordinary lengths to avoid having to teach any of the children on the island **anything**.

Whenever Ned reluctantly rolled himself over to Madame Sloth's house for his weekly lesson, she would not utter a single word to him. Instead, she would look at him haughtily and open her hand to be paid. Once her palm had been crossed with silver, she would waddle over to her old gramophone, and put on a recording she had made of her giving a piano lesson. This was just in case any grown-ups were passing by her house and heard what she was really up to.

Which was, of course, nothing.

"Now, child, let Madame Sloth hear those scales one more time," the voice on the crackly old record would say.

Then you would hear the sound of piano keys being struck.

PLONK! PLONK! PLONK!

Once the illusion had been created, Madame Sloth would take an hour-long snooze on the chaise longue.

"**ZZZZ!**
ZZZZ!
ZZZZ!"

The only way she would wake herself up in that time was with one of her own **bottom bangers.**

BABOOM!

They were as thunderous as a Wagner opera.

If her bottom bangers didn't wake her, an ornate gold carriage clock on her mantelpiece would chime to tell her the hour was up and her lesson was over.

CHING!

How was Madame Sloth allowed to get away with this? Because Greta Greed did nothing about it. In fact, she encouraged it. Anything that brought children misery was fine by her.

Because Ned never learned a thing about playing the piano in his years of enduring Madame Sloth's "piano lessons", he would be sent off to have more and more lessons!

One day when his mother returned home from the fish market, Ned told her what was really happening in those lessons.

NOTHING.

NOWT.

NADA.

N U F F I N K .

DIDDLY SQUAT.

Of course, being a grown-up, Ned's mother didn't believe him. Just like all the other grown-ups on the island, Madame Sloth had bamboozled the woman into thinking she was the most fantabulous piano teacher in the world.

Aside from her gramophone scam, Madame Sloth had a trio of nasty tricks up the sleeve of her long, flowery blouse.

If a child dared to complain about the daylight robbery, Madame Sloth would open the piano lid and shut the nasty little wretch inside.

C L A N G!

That way, Madame Sloth could carry on with her precious snooze undisturbed.

"LET ME OUT!"

"ZZZZ! ZZZZ! ZZZZ!"

If a child attempted to grass her up to their parents, in the next lesson Madame Sloth would turn the piano stool upside down and make them perch on one of the legs for the full hour!

"OUCH!"

If a child was so bold as to wake Madame Sloth up from one of her snoozes, they would be held upside down by their ankles and forced to play the piano with their nose.

"OUCH! OUCH! OUCH!"

PLONK! PLONK! PLONK!

One time, Ned couldn't take any more of this nonsense. As Madame Sloth lay on the sofa snoring and **bottom banging...**

"ZZZZ! ZZZZ! zzzz!"

...he shouted, "THIS IS THE END! I AM NEVER, EVER COMING TO ONE OF YOUR STUPID PIANO LESSONS EVER AGAIN!"

Needless to say, the piano teacher woke up in a FOUL mood. Without a word, Sloth walked out of the piano room and into the kitchen. As Ned sat on the piano stool, bemused, she returned clutching not one, not two, not three, but six tins of baked beans. One by one she ripped them open and guzzled them down in seconds like some kind of strongman at a fair. Her tummy began making the most disturbing sounds, like a boiler that was about to explode.

"I need to go!" announced Ned.

"Just one moment," replied Sloth.

Next, she shuffled over to the boy. From the way she shuffled, it was clear she was clenching her cheeks together. Not her top cheeks – her bottom cheeks. Then, as soon as her behind was close to Ned's nose, she unclenched.

"NOOOOOOOOO!" cried the boy.

Sloth let off the most explosive **BOTTOM BANGER** of all time.

KABOOM!

The force of the blast was enough to blow Ned straight out of the window.

WHOOSH

Needless to say, Ned was in no doubt as to how much he and all the children of the island had suffered at the hands of this monstrous woman. He knew that he would be doing them all a favour by teaching the teacher a lesson.

The question was,

how?

Chapter 19

DANCE TO THE MUSIC OF SLIME

It may surprise you to know that for someone who taught the piano, Madame Sloth could not actually play the piano herself. Not a note. In fact, she hated the sound of a piano being played, as she did all musical instruments.

The only sound she did like was the SOUND OF SILENCE.

Silence meant Sloth could sleep in peace.

As Ned and **Slime** flew over the island, Ned spotted the roof of Madame Sloth's grand old black-and-white house. It was easy to spot as she had a swimming pool the shape of a piano in the garden – no doubt paid for by her ill-gotten gains.

"There!" exclaimed the boy.

The pair swooped down to the ground beside the house. Looking through the window – surprise, surprise – they saw that the piano

teacher, if you could call her that, was fast asleep on her chaise longue, snoring away.

"ZZZZ! ZZZZ! ZZZZ!"

Looking across the piano room, Ned and **Slime** could see the child Sloth was meant to be teaching. The poor thing had been made to stand on one leg on the piano stool whilst balancing a book of sheet music on her head. Presumably this was some kind of punishment, no doubt for daring to stand up to the world's laziest piano teacher.

The pigeons set Ned down and **trans-slimed** back into a blob.

The girl balancing on the stool looked as if she were about to expire. Her face had gone as red as a tomato, and she was pouring with sweat. She must have been balancing there like a flamingo for nearly an hour.

With a nod of his head, Ned signalled to her that she should escape.

"Are you sure?" the girl mimed. She was clearly terrified of the lady sprawled out on the chaise longue.

Ned nodded his head again.

Tentatively, the girl put her other leg down and breathed a gigantic sigh of relief.

"Thank you!" she mouthed, before tiptoeing out of the room.

Slime slid under the boy's feet and inflated into a ball so Ned was just the right height to slide in through Sloth's open window.

The boy eased himself through, landing on a piano stool. The **slimeball** followed. At first it was too fat to fit through.

SHUNT! SHUNT! SHUNT!

Then **Slime** made itself thin and poured itself through.

SQUELCH!

"Shush!" shushed Ned. "Let's not wake Sloth. Yet!"

How best to wake someone who loves silence?

With the world's loudest noise, of course!

"**Slime!**" began the boy breathlessly. His idea was so good he couldn't get it out quick enough.

"**Yes?**" replied **Slime,** now turning back into a blob in the piano room.

"I need you to become the hugest orchestra in the world."

"Goody! Goody!"

"And I want you to make the noisiest noise that ever –" Ned wasn't sure of the word, so guessed at one – **"NOISED".** *

This was perfect payback for Sloth's explosive **bottom banger.**

---

* *A word you will most definitely find in perhaps the most important book ever published,* **The** Walliamsictionary.

In an instant, the blob divided into a hundred smaller blobs. These small blobs, smaller than **globules,** are called **"globettes"**.* One by one, the **globettes** began to take shape.

These **globettes trans-slimed** into musical instruments faster than Ned could name them.

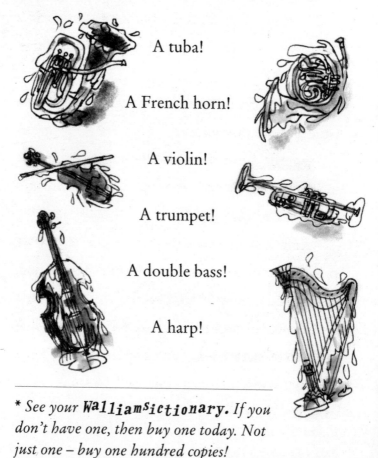

A tuba!

A French horn!

A violin!

A trumpet!

A double bass!

A harp!

---

* See your **Walliamsictionary**. *If you don't have one, then buy one today. Not just one – buy one hundred copies!*

A set of cymbals!

A xylophone!

A bass drum!

And, last but
not least, a giant gong!

Madame Sloth was oblivious, still snoozing
on her chaise longue.

"ZZZZ! ZZZZ! ZZZZ!"

"Now, orchestra," began Ned, "gather around
her, and I will conduct!"

When all the pieces of the orchestra were in
position, as close to the piano teacher as possible,
Ned assumed the role of conductor. He picked
up a banana from the fruit bowl on the coffee
table to use as a baton. The boy had once seen a
conductor on the television, so had some sense
of what to do.

Ned tapped the banana on the table to get the attention of all the slimy instruments.

TAP! TAP! TAP!

Still Madame Sloth snored and trumped away.

"ZZZZ! ZZZZ! zzzz!"

PFT! PFFFTT! PFFFFFT!

Her **bottom bangers** were so foul they could strip the wallpaper from the walls.

All the instruments in the **slime** orchestra (or **"slimechestra"***) turned to the conductor. Ned nodded and twirled his banana through the air.

---

* *I have to admit some of these are better than others, but you will find them all in your* Walliamsictionary.

The noisiest noise that ever noised exploded into the room.

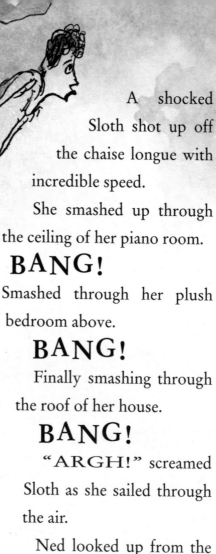

A shocked Sloth shot up off the chaise longue with incredible speed.

She smashed up through the ceiling of her piano room.

BANG!

Smashed through her plush bedroom above.

BANG!

Finally smashing through the roof of her house.

BANG!

"ARGH!" screamed Sloth as she sailed through the air.

Ned looked up from the piano stool through the hole in the roof.

The boy smiled to himself before he

remembered   something
he had learned.

Something important.

Sir Isaac Newton's Law of
Universal Gravitation.

In short – what goes up must
come down.

"ARGH!" screamed Sloth
again, not that screaming did
any good, but it seemed like the
appropriate thing to do.

The large lady was plummeting
straight towards little Ned. If
the boy didn't do something – and
fast – he would be nothing more than
human **slime!**

"HHHEEELLLP!" screamed
Ned. Now he was screaming too.
"THE PIANO!"

Thinking fast, **Slime trans-slimed**
back into a blob and reached round

the legs of Madame Sloth's grand piano with its blobby arms. It yanked the instrument under the hole in the roof, knocking Ned on his piano stool out of the way as it did so.

"ARGH!" screamed Sloth, before crash-landing into her own grand piano!

KLANG!

KLUNG! KLING!

SMASH!

BANG! WALLOP!

"My piano!" she cried from inside the mess of wood and keys and wire. "Now I can't give any more piano lessons!"

"You never did!" retorted the boy.

"NED!" she screamed. "I WILL GET YOU FOR THIS!"

With that, Sloth tried to lift herself up from her piano. In all the kerfuffle, the gold carriage clock toppled off her mantelpiece. It clonked Sloth on the head.

BOINK!

"OUCH!" she cried.

"Another job well done!" remarked Ned.

"Always a pleasure!" replied **Slime**, as it **trans-slimed** into a rocket. **"HOP ON!"**

The boy smiled and hauled himself up.

Then the rocket blasted him through the hole in Sloth's ceiling, high into the sky above.

ZOOM!

"I got the *ZOOMIES!*" howled the boy in delight.

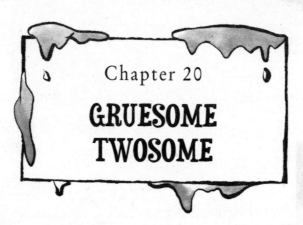

Chapter 20

GRUESOME TWOSOME

Glutton's Glaces was the name emblazoned on the island's one and only ice-cream van.

The proprietors were a husband-and-wife team, Glen and Glenda Glutton. They were meant to sell ice cream, but instead they ate it. All of it. Every last bit.

The technique they had for stealing from children was foolproof.

The van would be parked up outside the playground, or school, or beach. Anywhere on the island where children could be found. Then Mrs Glutton would appear at the serving window.

"What delicious ice cream would you like, my dear?" she would ask in her nice voice. She had a nice one and a nasty one. More of the nasty one in a moment.

"Oooh!" Ned cooed, looking at the sign with all the delicious toppings.

"Take your time, my dear."

"A Mr Whippy with chocolate sauce and chocolate chips and a chocolate flake, please!" Ned really liked chocolate.

"Wonderful choice, my dear. Now, money first!"

"Can you change a one-pound note, please?" asked the boy. It had been a Christmas present from his grandmother.

"Of course we can, my dearest of dears!"

As soon as Ned had passed the money over, she snatched it out of his hand and yelled, "MR GLUTTON! **DRIVE!**" This was in her nasty voice.

Glen Glutton, who'd been sitting in the driving seat all along, then put his foot down on the accelerator pedal and they sped off.

BRUMM!

As they did, the pair shouted, "SO LONG, SUCKER!"

Poor Ned was left at the side of the road in a cloud of burning rubber smell from the tyres.

With no ice cream.

And no pound note.

How could the Gluttons be allowed to get away with this?

Greta Greed, of course. There had been so many attempts to bring the pair to justice, but Greed stepped in every time to prevent them from being arrested. To think that this awful duo had made so many children miserable caused the old lady's dark heart to sing with joy. The **ISLE OF MULCH** often had visitors, providing fresh victims for the Gluttons.

The gruesome twosome were not the best advertisements for their own ice cream. Both ate so much of it, straight from the pump, that their teeth had turned black or fallen out altogether. Sometimes a rotten tooth would fly out mid-sentence and hit a child on the head.

P I N G !

Because they ate so much ice cream, Glen and Glenda Glutton had ballooned. So much so that they never left their van.

They couldn't!

It was impossible for them to fit through the doors!

So the Gluttons slept in the van, they ate in the van, they even did their doo-dahs in the van.

Just don't ask for the chocolate sprinkles. They don't smell anything like chocolate.

As Ned zoomed over the island on his "slocket",* he spotted a long line of children. They were from the posh boarding school on the **ISLE OF TWADDLE.**

Their hideous purple-and-yellow blazers gave them away.

The pupils must have been on a trip to see the world's most boring tourist attraction, **MULCH'S MEDIEVAL FORT.** It was a ruin, little more than a few old stones jutting

---

* *The Walliamsictionary is never wrong.*

out of the ground. Because it was old, grown-ups decided that children had to go and look at it. Often for hours at a time.

"DIVE!" ordered the boy.

Still riding the **slocket**, he hovered over the heads of the children. They were too sad to even crack a smile at a rocket made of slime.

"What happened?" Ned called out from above.

"It was those **rotten** ice-cream sellers," sobbed one.

"They took a mammoth order of ice creams from our whole school and made off with all our pocket money," blubbered another.

"The pair were so rude they shouted, 'SO LONG, SUCKERS!' as they sped off in their dirty old van," snuffled a third.

"We thought having ice cream would help us get over the crushing disappointment of having visited the world's dullest tourist attraction," bawled a fourth. "But we were wrong."

"It's made this school trip the worst day out ever," yowled a fifth.

"I would actually prefer to be at

TWADDLE COLLEGE FOR NOBLE OFFSPRING

right now doing double Mathematics!"

"Surely nothing is worse than double Mathematics!" exclaimed Ned.

"This is," replied the previous child, before bursting into floods of tears. "Boo! Hoo!"

This set all the Twaddle children off again.

"BOO! HOO! HOO!"

It was a symphony of sobbing.

"These kids are really annoying," murmured **Slime.**

"Shush!" shushed Ned, before turning to the children to ask, "Which way did the gruesome twosome go?"

All of the children were bawling their eyes out, actually unable to speak.

"Oh, for goodness' sake!" muttered **Slime.** "SHUSH!"

Instead the children pointed.

Fortunately, all in the same direction.

"Thank you, kids! **Slime!** That way!" ordered Ned, and he zoomed off. "I'll be back, Twaddlers!"

"BOO! HOO! HOO!"

The **ISLE OF MULCH** was a network of long windy country roads sheltered by trees, so it was difficult to spot vehicles from above.

But then **Glutton's Glaces** was no ordinary vehicle.

This great pink monstrosity, with a giant model of a Mr Whippy ice cream on its roof, would be visible from outer space. Soon the van rolled into view, and Ned signalled for **Slime** to zoom down beside it.

At first Mr and Mrs Glutton didn't see the strange sight of a boy riding a slocket zooming beside them.

Glen was in the driving seat, devouring a **HUMONGOUS** handful of ice cream with a flake sticking out.

Ned tapped on the driver's window to get the brute's attention.

At first Glen smiled and nodded back, before the surreal display made him slam on the brakes.

SCREECH!

The ice cream he was scoffing went everywhere.

All over his face.

SPLAT!

And all over the windscreen.

S P L U T !

Meanwhile, in the back, Mrs Glutton had been counting the cash she'd stolen from the **TWADDLE** children. Because of the sudden stop she found herself upside down on the floor of the van.

"HELP ME, YOU FOOL!" she cried out to her husband, unable to pull herself up to stand.

"I CAN'T SEE!" shouted Mr Glutton as he scrambled over his seat into the back of the van. As he did so, his huge foot knocked the tap on the ice-cream pump.

SPLURGE!

Mr Whippy began swamping them.

"ARGH!" cried Mrs G. "My botty is frozen!"

Still blind from having a face full of ice cream, Mr G tripped over his wife and fell right on top of her.

"OOF!" he cried.

"OUCH!" she cried. "GET OFF ME, YOU GREAT LUMP!"

"I AM NOT A GREAT LUMP!"

"NO! I AM SORRY. I GOT IT WRONG. YOU ARE A MASSIVE LUMP!"

Ned, who was still hovering outside the window, burst out laughing.

"HA! HA! HA!"

"SOMEONE'S LAUGHING AT US!" barked Mr Glutton.

"THEY ARE REALLY GOING TO GET IT!"

bawled Mrs Glutton.

Chapter 21
PEEVED COW

Mrs Glutton shoved her lump of a husband off her and scrambled to her feet. Next she shut off the ice-cream tap, which had still been splurging away.

CLICK!

"It's Ned," announced Ned, still hovering outside their van on his **slocket**. "Remember me?"

The boy was sure the pair would, after so cruelly stealing his pound note.

"No!" barked Glenda. "Should I?"

"Yes!" said the boy, miffed that he hadn't been remembered.

"I know you!" began Glen.

Ned smiled. "Go on…!"

"Aren't you the boy who was just flying by the window?"

"YES!" snapped Ned. "But I mean before then! Obviously!"

"You don't ring any bells," muttered Glenda.

"I am Ned. I ordered a Mr Whippy. I gave you a pound note. You just stole it and sped off! No ice cream. No nothing!"

Mr and Mrs Glutton looked at each other.

"Sorry, still no. Not a clue," said Mrs Glutton.

"To be honest," began Mr G, "we do that all day, every day, so try as we might we can't remember individual victims."

"Don't take it to heart, boy," chirped Mrs G, licking Mr Whippy off her chin with her thick, rough tongue.

If this was meant to pacify Ned, it had the opposite effect. The boy became enraged.

"Well, I am going to get my revenge on the pair of you! For me, and the hundreds of other children you have robbed."

The pair looked at each other and burst out laughing.

"HA! HA! HA!"

"Hundreds?" began Mr Glutton. "It's more like thousands!"

"Millions!" his wife chuckled.

"Billions!"

"Trillions!"

"Zillions!"

"HA! HA! HA!"

"Well, I, Ned, am going to use my

SLIMEPOWER

for all of them!" announced Ned.

"Your what?" grunted Glen.

"The boy is bananas," grunted Glenda.

"Your crime spree is over!"

"You'll have to catch us first!" exclaimed Mr Glutton. With that, he hauled himself on to the driving seat and stamped on the accelerator pedal.

STOMP!

BRRRRRRMMM!

"SO LONG, SUCKER!" they shouted.

The ice-cream van lurched off…

SCREECH!

…toppling Mrs Glutton off her feet again.

"OOF!" she cried as she landed on her ample bottom.

The problem was that the windscreen was

STILL covered in ice cream.

Mr Glutton couldn't see a thing.

As a result, the van skidded off the road.

SCREECH!

Smashed through a hedge.

CRUNCH!

Then bumped its way
across a field of cows.

BUMP!
 BUMP!
  BUMP!

"MOO! MOO! MOO!" cried the cows, as well you might if an ice-cream van was speeding straight at you, and, of course, you were a cow.

"WATCH WHERE YOU'RE GOING, YOU FOOL!" yelled Mrs Glutton, bouncing up and down in the back.

"I CAN'T SEE A BLASTED THING!" yelled Mr Glutton.

He flicked on the windscreen wipers.

SWISH! **SWASH!** *SWISH!* **SWASH!**

"THE ICE CREAM WON'T COME OFF!" he bellowed.

"THAT'S BECAUSE IT'S ON THE INSIDE, YOU IGNORAMUS!" Mrs Glutton bellowed back.

The man shook his head and wiped the inside of the windscreen with his sleeve.

At last he could see! But the sight that greeted Mr Glutton made him shriek with horror.

"AAARRRGHHH!"

On Ned's suggestion, **Slime** had formed into a giant Mr Whippy ice cream. The boy was the topping!

"REMEMBER ME NOW?" called Ned.

The ice-cream van was heading straight for it.

"STILL NO!" barked Mr Glutton. He was driving too fast to make the van stop!

He stamped on the brake hard.

STOMP!

So hard that the back wheels jumped up into the air.

WHOOSH!

It somersaulted over the giant Mr Whippy before crash-landing upside down on the grass.

KERTHUMP!

"MOO!" cried the cows as they scattered out of the way.

Slime trans-slimed back into a blob, placing Ned on to the back of a peeved-looking cow.

"MOO!"

Ned patted the cow. "Good girl!"

"WE'LL GET YOU FOR THIS, BOY!" shouted an upside-down Mr Glutton.

"WE'LL GET YOU GOOD AND PROPER!" agreed an upside-down Mrs Glutton.

Then the boy gave the cow a gentle slap, and it trotted closer to the ice-cream van. "Well, seeing as you love ice cream so much, I thought you might like to try the special **slime** flavour."

"**SLIME** FLAVOUR?" bawled Glen.

"SOUNDS DISGUSTING!" bawled Glenda.

"It is!" replied the boy. "**Slime!** Let's give the good Mr and Mrs Glutton a humongous helping!"

"A splendid idea, Ned," it said, before **oozing** through the gap in the window.

"NOOOOOOO!" the pair screamed as goo began filling their upturned van.

Still the slime **oozed** and **oozed** in, until the entire upside-down ice-cream van was full to bursting.

Then the windscreen, windows and the doors exploded with the pressure.

CRACK!
SMASH!
BOOM!

The van broke into pieces.

CLATTER!

CLATTER!

CLATTER!

The gruesome twosome **oozed** out on to the cowpat-covered grass in a giant puddle of **slime** (or "**sluddle**"*).

"EURGH!" moaned Mrs Glutton. "I am all slimy!"

"What's he done to our van?" cried Mr Glutton.

---

* "Sluddle" could also mean "slime cuddle", so be careful when using it in everyday speech. If in doubt, consult your **Walliamsictionary.**

"Slime! Seize their ice cream!" ordered Ned.

"Goody! Goody!" replied the blob as it gathered itself back together.

"NOO!" cried the pair.

"We've barely eaten today!" said Mr G.

"We are starving!" added Mrs G.

But **Slime** was quick and had soon pulled the huge metal ice-cream dispenser out of the wreck of the van.

CLUNK!

"We have some hungry children to feed!" Ned announced. **"Let's fly."**

Slime became a giant airship or "SLIMEPPELIN"* and picked up the boy from the back of the grateful cow.

"MOO!"

Then it whisked Ned and the ice-cream dispenser high into the sky.

---

* *A genius merging of the words "slime" and "Zeppelin", the old German airship named after its inventor, proving that* **The Walliamsictionary** *is an excellent educational tool.*

"WE'LL GET YOU…!" began Mr Glutton.
"WHAT'S YOUR NAME AGAIN?"
"SO LONG, SUCKERS!" called back Ned.

Chapter 22

ICE-CREAM PARTY

The kids from **TWADDLE SCHOOL FOR NOBLE OFFSPRING** were still boo-hoo-hooing beside the ruin when Ned returned in his airship made of slime.

"BOO! HOO! HOO!"

"KIDS!" called out Ned. "I told you I would be back! And I've brought ice cream!"

"YES!" they all cheered as **Slime** and Ned descended. **Slime** set the ice-cream dispenser down on a boring block of stone that the grown-ups claimed was once part of **MULCH'S MEDIEVAL FORT.**

The posh children all rushed over to the big metal box of Mr Whippy.

"ICE CREAM!" they cried. "YAHOO!"

Slime was now back to its **blobulous** self, sitting next to Ned on a mossy stone. The friends shared a smile at another job well done.

In an instant, the cheers of the children turned to silence.

"Excuse me, but where are the cones?" asked one.

"Oh, sorry, we didn't think to bring any cones," replied Ned, rather taken aback.

"And I am partial to a chocolate flake," remarked another.

"Well, we didn't really have time to—"

"And the hundreds and thousands?" enquired a third.

"**Ungrateful little—**" began **Slime**.

"Shush!" shushed Ned.

"BOO! HOO! HOO!" they all bawled together.

"NOW WE ARE NOT GOING TO HAVE

ANY ICE CREAM!" moaned one.

"THIS TRIP HAS GONE FROM BAD TO WORSE!" whined another.

"TAKE ME BACK TO DOUBLE MATHS!" whimpered a third.

Slime rolled its eyes. **"I've got a good mind to take that ice-cream dispenser, and shove it—"**

"SHUSH!" shushed Ned. "Look, kids, all you have to do is flick the nozzle and it's… AN ICE-CREAM PARTY!"

Ned did just that…

CLICK!

…and the soft white Mr Whippy ice cream splurged out.

SPLURGE!

It splurged all over Ned.

SPLURGE!

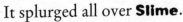

It splurged all over **Slime**.

SPLURGE!

It splurged all over the children.

SPLURGE!

It splurged all over **MULCH'S MEDIEVAL FORT.**

In no time, everyone was covered in the stuff! They looked like snowmen!

"ICE-CREAM PARTY!" cried one, licking the ice cream off her nose.

"THIS IS THE BEST DAY EVER!" cried another, scooping handfuls of ice cream off the top of her head and shoving them in her mouth.

"I still would have liked a flake," muttered a third, tearfully.

"I am dairy intolerant," remarked a fourth.

"Is there a vegan option?"

"You can't please everyone," muttered Ned to **Slime**.

"**It certainly seems that way,**" it replied. "**Where next, my friend? The day is coming to an end.**"

Ned instantly knew where. "Everything today has been leading up to this. This is the last one. And it is going to be dangerous."

"**Goody! Goody! I love danger!**" **Slime** replied.

Chapter 23

FLYING SAUCER

"**A**re you allergic to cats?" asked Ned. It was an important question. Aunt Greta had 101 of them.

"Not that I know of," said **Slime**.

"Then let's go!" exclaimed the boy.

"Do you have a preferred mode of transport?"

"Surprise me!"

Slime smiled, and **trans-slimed** into a flying saucer.

"A flying saucer!" exclaimed Ned as he watched the thing spin and spin.

"I suppose I was thinking of cats. Cats drink out of saucers!"

"You are clever."

"**I know!**" agreed **Slime**.

"Let's go!"

Slime plucked the boy from the fort and placed him on top of the flying saucer.

"**Which way, Ned?**" it asked.

The boy was spinning round on top of the saucer and beginning to feel more than a little dizzy. However, he could see his aunt's colossal castle sitting proudly on the tallest hill on the island.

"THAT WAY!" he said, pointing in every direction.

"**You mean the castle?**" asked **Slime**.

"YES!"

"So, who lives there?"

"The person who owns this wretched island. The one who loathes children more than anyone, my Aunt Greta."

"She sounds delightful!" joked **Slime**.

"Delightful is not the first word that springs to mind."

"So I take it you are not close?"

"Close? Ha! Ha! I haven't seen Aunt Greta in a long, long time!"

"Well then, we need to pop by!"

The **Slime** flying saucer spun faster and faster through the sky, with poor Ned clinging on for dear life.

WHIRR!

Chapter 24
KITTY LITTER CASTLE

There are cat ladies, and there are CAT LADIES. Aunt Greta Greed was a CAT LADY. She had over a hundred of them. Aunt Greta and her 101 cats (I told you she had over one hundred) lived in a remote castle. It stood high on a hill overlooking the entire **ISLE OF MULCH,** which she owned. Because of her obsession with cats, Aunt Greta had named her home KITTY LITTER CASTLE.

The grand old lady wore long flowing dresses dotted with images of cats. Whenever she walked, she clanked, because she was drowning in jewellery.

All Aunt Greta's jewellery was, of course, cat-themed.

 Cat brooches.

 Cat earrings.

Cat bracelets. Cat rings.

Cat watches.

 Cat pendants.

She even had a cat tiara, a crazy cat crown!

On her walls the lady had the most extraordinary collection of artwork, as long as you liked cats. The cats were often rendered in re-creations of famous paintings.

The Mona Moggy

The Cat's Scream

Pussy with a Pearl Earring

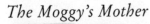

The Moggy's Mother

The Son of Cat

Pussy Portrait
with a
Bandaged Ear

The Laughing
Catalier

The Cat's Kiss

The Cat's Luncheon
on the Grass

Cat Leading the Cats

But there weren't just paintings of cats. Oh no. There were also statues of cats everywhere, in bronze, silver and gold.

239

Here was a statue of a cat playing with a ball of wool.

Here was another of one curled up asleep.

She even had one of a cat licking its own bottom.

As Aunt Greta had 101 cats, she couldn't possibly remember that many names. So she decided to name every single one of them **Tiddles**.

"**Tiddles!** It's dinnertime!" she would call, and 101 cats would charge towards her, sweeping her off her feet.

Cats were Aunt Greta's only friends.

The lady didn't like people. She didn't trust them. Even though Ned was her nephew, she never, ever saw him, or her niece, Jemima, or even her younger sister, their mother. That is because Greta had come into a large inheritance from a long-lost relative. It was millions upon millions upon millions.

And Greed wasn't sharing a penny of it with anybody!

There was a huge sign outside the castle that read:

TRESPASSERS WILL BE EATEN.
BY CATS.

If this wasn't enough to put you off trying to get in, then the lack of a drawbridge over the moat might. Years ago, Aunt Greta Greed burned it, and it sank into the water below. With no drawbridge to the castle, nobody could come near. Greed could be left all alone with her riches. And, of course, her cats.

These pampered creatures sported sparkling diamond-encrusted collars, devoured caviar (fish eggs, which might not sound expensive, but which are hideously so), and slept on silk sheets in four-poster beds.

In the event of her death, Aunt Greta was planning to leave KITTY LITTER CASTLE and all its contents to – you've guessed it – her cats.

There were times when those close to Aunt Greta begged for her to help them.

For a morsel of food.

For somewhere to sleep for the night.

For a penny to help anybody, even those in desperate need.

Even Ned, when he needed some new tyres

for his wheelchair, had been spurned by his wicked aunt. As were all the children of the island. One day a group of children plucked up the courage to ask, "Please may we play a game of football on one of the fields you own?"

Without a word to them, Aunt Greta set her 101 cats on the children.

"TIDDLES! ATTACK!"

"MIAOW!"
"HISS!"
SCRATCH!

Needless to say, the children never asked again.

But they **never** forgot her cruelty.

And neither did Ned.

Chapter 25

A SWARMING SEA OF CATS

The **Slime** flying saucer or **USO** (Unidentified Sliming Object) spun through the sky. It spun so fast that poor Ned couldn't hold on any longer. One by one Ned could feel his fingers lose their grip. As the **USO** flew over KITTY LITTER CASTLE, the boy felt himself flying through the air.

"ARGH!" he screamed.

Slime chased after him, but Ned was spinning so fast it couldn't catch him.

He tumbled through the air into the castle's moat.

sPLOSH!

The boy sank deep under the water. He couldn't swim. Unless **Slime** did something, and fast, Ned would be no more.

Slime dived down into the moat and came back up as some kind of sea monster with a soaked Ned riding on its back.

Needless to say, as it was wet, the monster was ssslippery too! Ned couldn't hold on. "WHOA!" he cried as he slid down the monster's back.

Just as he was about to fall off completely, the monster swished its tail and sent the boy flying through the air.

WHOOSH!

"WHOA!"
Ned flew straight over the wall of the castle.

"AAAAHHHH!"
Below him, Ned could see the castle courtyard getting nearer and nearer.

It was a swarming sea of cats!

Cats of every size and colour!

Black cats, white cats, ginger cats, grey cats, red cats, blue cats, even one of those weird baldy cats.

"MIAOW!" "MIAOW!" "MIAOW!"

Any moment now, the boy was going to land right on top of them.

"HELP!" he screamed.

"CATS!"

"HISS!"

"HISS!" "HISS!"

Chapter 26
EATEN ALIVE

As Ned tumbled through the air, he shut his eyes tight. The boy was about to be eaten alive by 101 cats. However, what Ned didn't see was that **Slime** was arching up from the moat to form a bouncy castle beneath him.

A bouncy castle made of slime.

A *"slouncy"* * castle.

This **slouncy** castle landed right on top of the cats.

"MIAOW!" "MIAOW!" "HISS!" "HISS!" "MIAOW!" "HISS!"

---

* **Walliamsictionary** *has this so just back off.*

Ned landed in the dead centre of the **slouncy** castle.

BOING!

Only to find himself flying back up into the air.

WHOOSH!

Back over the wall.

WHOOSH!

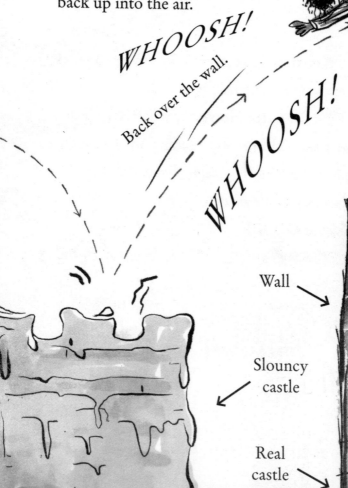

Wall

Slouncy castle

Real castle

Heading straight for the moat again!

Once Ned had been plucked from the murky depths, **Slime** turned itself into a ladder. A "sladder".*

A sladder seemed like the perfect way to get over the castle wall. That was until the boy actually attempted to haul himself up with his arms. It was so wet and ssslippery he ssslid sssstraight back down into the moat.

SPLOSH!

---

* Walliamsictionary.
Come on, guys. Get with the beat.

Eventually, after much discussion between Ned and his slimy friend, a solution was found.

It was so simple it was brilliant.

The boy would be shot out of a **slime** cannon (or **"slannon"***) and land on top of KITTY LITTER CASTLE.

So, on the count of three…

"One, two, three!"

…**Slime** blasted Ned up into the air.

BANG!

WHOOSH!

Over the wall of the castle.

WHOOSH!

Over the courtyard of cats.

WHOOSH!

Over the other wall of the castle.

WHOOSH!

Crash-landing in the moat on the far side.

SPLOSH!

---

* *I am not telling you again.*

N O O O O O O !

Slime trans-slimed back into the sea monster and plunged down into the depths of the moat to save his friend.

Once back on dry land, the boy wailed, "THIS IS IMPOSSIBLE!"

"**Nothing is impossible**," replied **Slime**.

"Getting into Aunt Greta's castle is!"

"**Yes, apart from that. Obviously.**"

"Obviously."

The pair thought for a moment.

"There must be some way over the wall and past those cats," said Ned.

"**What do cats hate?**" asked **Slime**.

"Dogs!"

"**Then a dog I shall be!**"

In an instant, **Slime trans-slimed** into a dog, or "**slog**".*

** Right. That's it. Question me one more time and this book will turn into **slime** in your hands!*

The **slog,** which was a hundred times the size of a normal dog, dried itself off by doing that weird shaking thing that dogs do.

F L U T T E R !

Next, the **slog** placed Ned on its back. Miraculously, the boy didn't **ssslip** off. It then paced away from the castle, before bounding towards it and taking a gigantic jump.

LEAP!

They leaped over the wall.

WHOOSH!

And... SUCCESS!

They landed in the castle courtyard, right on top of the sea of cats.

"MIAOW!" "MIAOW!" "MIAOW!!" "HISS!" "HISS!" "HISS!" "HISS!"

With cats circling them, the pair were scared.

"W-w-what sh-sh-shall w-w-we d-d-do?" asked **Slime**.

"YOU ARE A DOG!" reminded Ned. "GROWL AT THEM!"

"I'll try," replied **Slime**. **"GRRRR!"**

Aunt Greta's cats were not easily scared. In fact, they actually laughed at this pitiful display.

"ME-How-How-How!"*

"Oh no," said Ned.

"Oh yes," said **Slime**.

The cats began circling the intruders, before going on the attack, baring their fangs.

"Hiss!"

Some of the bolder cats began scratching at this "dog" with their claws.

"MiAow!"

"Hiss!"

SWIPE!

SCRATCH!

---

* *Yes, that is how cats laugh. I have heard them laughing when reading my books.*

Ned and **Slime** cowered in a corner. They cowered so far in the corner that in no time the pair were nothing more than a gooey mess.

"**Oh no!**" exclaimed **Slime**.

"Oh yes!" exclaimed Ned.

"**It looks like the end.**"

"It certainly does. There are just so many of them!"

"**How many?**" asked **Slime**.

"I can't count them all! They keep moving around!"

Still Aunt Greta's army of cats hissed and swiped with their claws.

"**MIAOW!**"

"**HISS!**"

S WIPE!

SCRATCH!

"If they aren't scared of dogs, there must be something else they are frightened of!" reasoned Ned.

"**But what?**"

The cats were pawing nearing and nearer.

STOMP! STOMP! STOMP!

"WATER!" exclaimed the boy.

"**Of course!**" agreed **Slime**.

"**Slime!** Become a raging sea! NOW!"

Slime did just as its friend asked. In no time at all, the castle courtyard was sloshing with a slimy sea (or *"slea"**).

"MMMMMIIAAooooowwwwww!"

screamed the cats.

---

* This is the worst one, I promise.

Ned was right. The cats were scared of water. In fact, they were TERRIFIED!

The monstrous moggies were now leaping on to anything floating on the surface of the slimy sea.

Chairs. Tables. Other cats.

"MMMIIAAoooWWW!"

Ned, who was body-surfing on a wooden tray, spied an open window on the wall.

"Through here, **Slime!**" he called out.

The boy slid through the window, and the sea of **slime** followed, pouring itself through the narrow frame.

Inside the castle, the boy fell on the floor.

THUD!

"OOF!"

The **slime** poured on top of him.

SPLURGE!

"YUCK!" said the boy.

Ned looked around. He was inside the biggest room he'd ever been in in his life. It was a picture of opulence. Oil paintings, priceless antiques, crystal chandeliers hanging from the ceiling. It was a world away from the humble cottage where he lived.

"WHO GOES THERE?" demanded a voice.

It was Ned's aunt, Greta Greed. The lady was standing right over them, dripping with jewels, and holding a particularly

fearsome cat

in her arms.

"HISS!"*

---

* *That was the cat, not Aunt Greta.*

Chapter 27

A CAT AS BIG AS A BEAR

At first glance, it wasn't clear who was holding who. It might as well have been the cat holding the aunt, as they were both the same size. The cat, like all the others, was called **Tiddles**. This **Tiddles** you could tell apart from all the rest for the simple reason that it was the

size of a grizzly bear. It was really **Gigantic Tiddles**.

"I SAID, 'WHO GOES THERE?'" repeated Aunt Greta.

The boy heaved himself up on to a chair. Meanwhile **Slime**, which had spread out all over the silk rug, gathered itself together again. It took its blobulous* form behind the boy.

---

* *It means blobbiful.***
** *It means blobulous.*

"It's me, Aunt Greta! Your favourite nephew – Ned!" spluttered the boy. "Well, I say 'favourite'… You've only got one. So I must be your favourite!"

Aunt Greta was not the least amused. "You are a leech is what you are, boy! Sucking all you can from me! Like the rest of your wretched family."

The evil cat was giving him the evil eye. They glinted like the diamonds on his collar.

"**HISS!**" it hissed.

"Didn't you read the sign? Trespassers will be eaten! I want you out of my castle now! Or I will set **Tiddles** on you!"

With that, she hurled **Gigantic Tiddles** towards the boy. The great thing landed with a thud on the floor.

DOOF!

"**HISS!**"

"And who is this gigantic bogey with you?" demanded Aunt Greta.

"**CHARMING!**" exclaimed **Slime**. As it looked down, it noticed that **Gigantic Tiddles** was licking **Slime's** blobby foot with its huge rough tongue. **Slime** did not agree with the cat one bit, and soon **Gigantic Tiddles** was coughing up not hairballs but **slimeballs**.

"HUH! HUH!"

"**Slime** is my friend," replied the boy.

"How perfectly **revolting** to have a lump of snot for a friend," remarked Aunt Greta.

"You should try having a friend someday, Aunt Greta. We worry about you here, all alone in your castle."

The lady chuckled to herself. "Ha! Ha! Friends? I have no need for friends. Or family. Or anybody. These are my nearest and dearest!"

With that, the lady displayed her jewels to the boy. Aunt Greta looked like a Christmas tree, with sparkly decorations dangling from every conceivable place.

Pearl earrings in the shape of cats

A ruby brooch with the face of a cat

A solid gold cat watch

Silver bracelet with cat charm on it

A sapphire pendant in the shape of a cat

And, of course, her crazy cat crown!

You might mistake Aunt Greta for a member of the royal family, if it were not for the stench of cat pee.

"What are you doing here, boy?" she sneered. "I didn't invite you to my castle. I never invite people to my castle. They always want something."

"Well, actually—" began Ned before he was cut off.

"Is it money? Is that why you are here? Because I will tell you now that you aren't getting a single penny of my millions! Do you hear me, boy? NOT A PENNY!"

"Is she always like this?" whispered **Slime.**

"This is her on a good day," replied Ned.

"What do you want, boy? Tell me!" she thundered. "Or else I will set my one hundred and one cats on you!"

Ned looked up at the castle window. The other hundred cats must have scrambled up the courtyard wall.

Now they were streaming into the living room. A rushing river of cats.

"Hiss!"

Led by **Gigantic Tiddles**, all the other **Tiddleses** began circling the pair, ready to strike.

"TELL ME, BOY!" she yelled, causing her jewellery to clank together. "OR YOU WILL BE CAT FOOD!"

"Miaow!"

"Hiss!"

The boy had the naughtiest notion. A notion that would teach this lady a lesson. A lesson that might just change the lives of all the children of **MULCH** forever.

"I am here, Auntie dearest, because I wanted to give you something."

The lady was intrigued. "ME?"

"Yes, you. I worry that you just don't have enough jewellery!"

Greta looked down at her many adornments.

"You are right, boy!" she trilled. "I don't have

nearly enough sparkly things. There is always a need for **more, more, MORE!**"

"Would you like some more?" asked Ned.

"YES!" growled Greed. "GIMME, GIMME, GIMME MORE!"

Ned looked at **Slime.** "I knew you would want more. Please! Let my friend **Slime** treat you!"

The pair smiled at each other. **Slime** knew exactly what to do.

"Let's start with another necklace!" exclaimed the boy.

With that, **Slime's** chest opened, and a torpedo of goo shot out.

SPLURGE!

It hit the lady's chest, covering her in **slime**.

SPLAT!

"URGH!"

"And, of course, some new earrings!"

Two smaller **slime** bombs struck her ears.

SPLAT! SPLAT!

"URGH!"

"And why have a tiara when you can have a great big massive crown?"

Then, what was left of **Slime** rose into the air, and came crashing down on her head, covering her from top to bottom in **GOO!**

SPLAT!

"EEEUUURRRGGGHHH!"

she shrieked.

As Ned allowed himself a chuckle…

"HA! HA! HA!"

…**Slime** gathered himself together again and shot back over to the boy.

"We need to get out of here!" exclaimed **Slime**.

"Why?"

"The Tiddleses are on the attack!"

Ned looked down. Surrounding him were cats, cats and more cats.

Leading the pride of cats was **Gigantic Tiddles**. The enormous beast jumped up at the boy, its fangs bared.

"HHHIIIssssss!"

Slime thought fast. Without a word it shot up to the ceiling.

SPLAT!

And stuck there.

It was now like a giant jellyfish. Long gooey tentacles poured down from above.

"What about me?" Ned called up.

"I am getting there!" Slime called down.

Just in time, the tentacles scooped up the boy and whisked him to the ceiling.

WHOOSH!

Ned's bare feet became embedded in the slime.

SPLUT!

He hung there, upside down, out of reach of the cats' claws, feeling more than a little pleased with himself.

However, the smug look on his face turned sour as his **slime-drenched** aunt barked her order.

"Tiddleses!
EAT THAT BOY!"

Chapter 28

A MOUNTAIN OF MOGGIES

Aunt Greta must have trained her 101 cats in circus skills – unlikely, I know, but stay with me – because immediately the beasts began climbing up on each other's shoulders. The cats formed some kind of cat ladder, or "cadder",* to give it its proper name.

---

* Come on, everyone knows this word!

In no time, the cats were rising. Higher and higher. In the blink of an eye, they were dangerously close to the boy, their sharp claws swiping at him.

SWISH!

SWISH!

SWISH!

"HISS!"

"SLIME! PLEASE! DO SOMETHING!"** Ned screamed.

Slime started sliming its way along the ceiling to escape.

SPLUT! SPLUT! SPLUT!

However, it soon became tangled up in a chandelier.

CHINK! CHANK! CHUNK!

"Tiddleses, WE HAVE THEM NOW!" bellowed Aunt Greta from below as she wiped the goo off her face. "ENJOY YOUR DINNER, MY BEAUTIES!"

Now cats are not the brightest of creatures. In my experience of spending time with different types of animals, I would rate their intelligence thus:

CHIMPANZEES

DOLPHINS

ELEPHANTS

PARROTS

RATS

CROWS

DOGS

PIGEONS

PIGS

OCTOPUSES

CATS

The not-clever thing that the cats did was make the kitten **Tiddleses** go at the bottom of the cat ladder, then the fully grown **Tiddleses** go in the middle, then the **Gigantic Tiddles** at the top. **Gigantic Tiddles** was now level with the boy, tangled up with **Slime** in the chandelier. The monstrous moggie was chomping at the air, just a whisker from Ned's face.

As **Slime** tried to escape from the chandelier...

"CHOMP! CHOMP! CHOMP!"

CLINK! CLANK! CLUNK!

...it accidentally swung the upside-down boy straight towards the beast.

W H O O S H !

"ARGH!" screamed Ned.

"CHOMP!" chomped **Gigantic**

Tiddles as its fangs bit into Ned's ear.

The pain was **eye-watering!**

"ARGH!"

What's more, the beast was not letting go!

"HHHEEELLLP!"

A giant cat earring is perhaps the most painful earring of them all.

The boy kept swinging, and **Gigantic Tiddles** swung too.

SWISH!

The beast swung so far that the cadder began to crumble.

"MiAow!"

"MiAow!"

"MiAow!"

As **Gigantic Tiddles** stayed locked on to Ned's ear with its fangs, the other hundred cats beneath him took a tumble, or "cumble".*

The hundred cats fell right on top of Aunt

---

* *A cat tumble. For goodness' sake, just buy* **The Walliamsictionary** *and be done with it.*

Greta.

THUD!

THUD!

THUD!

"MIAOW!"

"MIAOW!"

"MIAOW!"

The lady was buried under a mountain of moggies.

"URGH!" came a muffled cry. No doubt one of the cats' bottoms (or **"cobboms"***) was stuck right under her nose.

With all the

---

* *A "cobbom" is an everyday word that requires zero explanation.*

other cats having tumbled (or "cumbled"*) to the floor, incredibly **Gigantic Tiddles** was still dangling (or "cangling"*) from Ned by his ear.

Try as Ned might to fight it off, the beast was not letting go of Ned's ear. In fact, it was sinking its fangs deeper and deeper into his flesh.

"CHOMP!"

"YEOW!" screamed Ned. As you might if you had a giant cat that weighed as much as a small car dangling from your ear.

Meanwhile, Aunt Greta was scrambling up from underneath the mountain of cats. Many of her moggies were still stuck all over her gooey body. The wicked lady looked like a huge furry monster.

---

* *Don't delay! Get your* **Walliamsictionary** *today!*

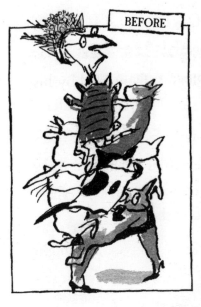

"I can't get this gigantic cat off my ear!" screamed Ned.*

"**Tickle it!**" suggested **Slime**.

"TICKLE IT?"

"**It's worth a try!**"

Immediately, the upside-down pair began tickling **Gigantic Tiddles** all over its body.

Its ears, its chin, its legs, its tummy, its tail.

---

* This is a sentence that, for all his centuries of acclaim, you will never find in a book by Charles Dickens.

TICKLE! TICKLE! TICKLE! TICKLE! TICKLE!

Nothing worked! The cat remained unmoved.

"TICKLE THE TIP OF ITS TAIL!" ordered Ned.

"I am not tickling the tip of a cat's tail!" replied **Slime**.

"Why not?" demanded the boy.

"People will talk!"

"Nonsense! Let's do it together!"

That is exactly what they did. The pair tickled the tip of **Gigantic** Tiddles's tail.

"ME! HOW! HOW!" the cat laughed. As it did so, it opened its mouth and let go of Ned's ear.

W H O O S H !

Gigantic **Tiddles** fell through the air.

"NNNNNOOOOO!" cried Aunt Greta from below as a cat the weight of a baby elephant crashed down on her head.

DOINK!

"OW!" she cried.

"Have you had enough now?" asked Ned. "Or would you like more, more, **more?**"

"Please!" pleaded Aunt Greta. "No more, more, **more!**"

"Then things have to change on **MULCH!**"

"Anything! Just name it!"

"No more nasty grown-ups terrorising children."

"I haven't a clue who you mean!" she protested.

"You know exactly who I mean! Wrath, the Envys, Pride, Sloth, the Gluttons. We children want them all off the island forever!"

"Or?" asked Greed.

"Or **Slime** will have its fun with you!"

"NOOOOO!" she begged. "I will have them shipped off at once!"

"Excellent!" exclaimed Ned. "And as for you…?"

"Well, I, er, I promise to be nicer to the nasty little wretches… I mean, children!"

"Mmm," mused the boy. "You are getting there. Now, please know you are welcome to be part of our family again. We would love you to pop over for tea at our cottage one day."

"Er-er-erm," stuttered the lady.

"Slime will take you!"

"It would be a pleasure," said **Slime** with a wicked tone in its voice. "Goody! Goody!"

"No to the lift, but yes for the tea," she replied.

"Super!" said Ned. "Now, **Slime,** let's go!"

Slime untangled itself from the chandelier to become a jet pack, or **"slet pack".***

---

* No explanation is needed. Nor will it be given.

"Goodbye for now!" said Ned.

Together the friends shot out of the castle window, and Aunt Greta watched them go, open-mouthed in shock.

ZOOOOOM!

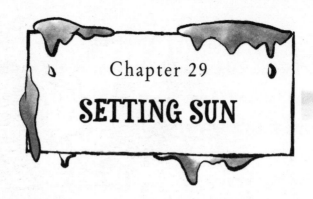

Chapter 29

SETTING SUN

It had been the most **slimetastic** day, but it was nearly over.

The sun was setting over **MULCH**.

"Home, please!" called out the boy to the slimy jet pack on his back.

"Certainly, Ned," obliged **Slime,** and they flew through the sky back to the place where the adventure had begun.

The family cottage.

W H O O S H !

Ned's home was eerily quiet from above. As it was only dusk, his mother and father would still be hard at work.

But where was his sister, Jemima?

Upon searching the whole house, Ned found that it was empty.

"Jemima!" he called out. "JEMIMA?"

But she was nowhere to be found.

"Where is she?" asked the boy.

Slime shook its slimy head. **"No idea. But she can't have gone far. Mulch isn't a big island."**

Checking in the bathroom, Ned noticed his wheelchair was missing too.

"My wheelchair! She's taken my wheelchair! My sister is an absolute horror. Where on earth has she put it?" he cursed.

"What would she want with it?"

"I bet she's thrown it off a cliff."

"Ned, you don't know that!"

"She's done worse!"

"Jemima can't be all bad."

"Oh, she is!" replied Ned.

"Well, let's see if we can find her! If we do, I am sure your wheelchair won't be far away."

"I guess so."

"I know so. Come on!"

With that, **Slime** scooped the boy out of the bathroom, and they took to the skies once more. This time, Ned's friend **trans-slimed** into a kite, or **"slite".***

The boy lay on top of the **slite,** and together they flew across the island in search of Jemima.

"LOOK!" shouted the boy. **"Boot prints!"**

---

* *Boring, I know. So boring it isn't even included in* **The Walliamsictionary.**

Indeed there were big boot prints in the mud leading into the forest.

The pair glided over the trees until Ned spotted a clearing. There was a flash of bright colours down below, and the boy thought it might just be his big sister's flowery dress. He gestured for **Slime** to descend, and silently the pair swooped down to the forest floor.

Slime changed back into being a blob. It scooped Ned up in its blobby arm, and held him tight.

The boy was right. Up ahead, beside the oldest tree in the forest, was Jemima. And his wheelchair. The girl was too far away for Ned to know what she was doing, but he was sure she was up to no good.

"Let's get her again!" Ned whispered to **Slime**.

"Hang on a moment," hesitated **Slime**.

"No! Come on! We need the element of surprise. Now turn yourself back into a ball."

"A slimeball?"

"Exactly! Then we can roll over to her, and – surprise! – cover her from head to toe in slime!"

Slime shrugged, as much as a blob of slime can shrug, and did what it was told.

Ned pulled himself on to the top of the **slimeball,** and together they rolled across the forest, nearer and nearer to the girl.

TRUNDLE! TRUNDLE! TRUNDLE!

It was only when they were near that Ned saw that Jemima's head was resting on the seat of his wheelchair. The boy wanted to tell her that he had blown off – countless times – on the very spot where her nose was, but thought better of it. It would spoil the surprise!

Rolling nearer still, Ned noticed Jemima was doing something he'd never heard her do before.

She was crying.

"Why is she blubbering?" whispered Ned to **Slime.**

"Maybe your sister misses you."

"Don't be daft, **Slime.** She hates me. Just like I hate her. Come on, let's get closer."

The **slimeball** rolled over a twig that snapped in two.

SNAP!

The noise must have startled Jemima. Acting on instinct, she leaped to her feet and kicked out. She kicked so hard with her booted foot…

BASH!

…that Ned and **Slime** shot up into the sky.

WHOOOSH!

"ARGH!" screamed the boy.

As he began tumbling back to earth, he realised this particular plan had not gone to, er, plan.

"SLIME!" he shouted up. "HELP ME!"

Slime was a great deal higher in the sky than him.

"NED! I CAN'T GET TO YOU!"

The boy screamed.

"ARGH!"

Ned was plummeting straight

towards Jemima.

Chapter 30

FOREVER

Then the most marvellous thing happened. Jemima caught Ned in her arms.

"OOF!" she exclaimed. "NED! I am so pleased I found you!"

Now face to face, Ned saw she had tears in her eyes.

Slime landed a little way off in the forest.

THUD!

It began rolling over towards them through the tall trees.

"Why were you crying, Jemima?" asked Ned.

"I was worried about you!" she replied, holding her little brother in her arms.

"Me?" The boy couldn't believe his ears.

"Yes. You. I am so sorry I made you run away from home."

"Well, you were always so beastly to me."

"I know. But I never wanted you to run away. When you did, I realised how much I…"

"You what?" asked Ned. Was Jemima really going to say it?

"…like you."

"I thought you were going to say 'love'."

"Let's stick with 'like' right now," replied Jemima.

"'Like' is good!" exclaimed Ned.

"You are my little brother and I should be

looking after you. Not playing horrid tricks on you."

"Thank goodness for that!" said Ned. "But why were you hiding out here in the forest?"

"Since dawn I have been looking all over the island for you. The forest was the last place I looked. I broke down, because night was falling, and I thought you were gone… forever."

By this time **Slime** had rolled all the way over to the pair.

TRUNDLE! TRUNDLE! TRUNDLE!

"Hello!" said **Slime.**

"AAAARRRGGGHHH!" screamed Jemima. "It talks!"

"There's no need to scream," reassured Ned.

"I am perfectly friendly," said **Slime**.

"You did boot me up the bottom!" said Jemima.

"Oh yes," replied **Slime**. **"Sorry about that."**

"I deserved it," she said. "But what are you?"

"I am Slime!"

Jemima lifted up her hand and touched this strange creature.

"Yes, you do feel very, very slimy," she remarked.

"Slime was made when I mixed together all those disgusting things you had collected in jars," added Ned.

Jemima's eyes fell. "So you found out about my little… plan?"

"Yes, I did," replied Ned.

"Oh no," she said.

"Oh yes. But because of all that I have made a friend and had the most marvellous adventure."

"Well. That's something, I guess. Where have you been?" she asked.

"Flying all over the island," replied **Slime**. **"We have been righting wrongs."**

"Well, I would like to right a wrong," began the girl. "Ned, I am sorry."

The boy smiled and wrapped his arms round his sister.

"Come with us," said Ned. "Let's take one last flight!"

"Me?" said Jemima.

"Yes! You!" said the boy. He took his sister by the hand. "One last time around the island, please, **Slime!**"

"**With pleasure**," replied **Slime**. It scooped up the pair and took to the sky. This time it changed into a great slimy dragon. Ned and Jemima held on to each other as they sat on its back, its wings flapping below them.

Chapter 31
FINAL FLIGHT

Together Ned and Jemima flew all over
MULCH.

They flew over the school, where the pupils
were all streaming out of the building, laughing
and joking. The children waved up to the three
in the sky.

"THANK YOU, NED!" they cried.

The boy beamed and waved back.

Next, they flew over the park.

To Ned's surprise,
a group of kids
were playing
football on the
grass.

"NED!"
they shouted up.
"WE LOVE
YOU!"

The boy beamed. "THANK YOU!" he called back.

Then they flew over the toyshop. Nearby a gaggle of children were out playing with their new toys.

"NED! YOU ARE THE BEST!" they shouted up.

Flying astride the dragon, the boy did a little bow.

"I've got a really cool brother!" remarked Jemima.

"Get used to it!" said Ned. "Ha! Ha!"

The pair chuckled as they flew over their mother's fish-market stall and waved to her.

"MUM! LOOK! WE ARE UP HERE!"

The poor woman fainted and fell into a tray of fish. As well you might faint if you saw your children flying on the back of a dragon made of **slime** (or "slime-a-gon"*).

Ned and Jemima swooped over their father's fishing boat that was just coming into port.

"DAD! LOOK!"

The man nearly tumbled off his boat into the sea.

"OOPS!" said Ned.

Another boat was heading out of port. It was a prison ship.

---

* *Not actually in* **The Walliamsictionary.**
Someone tell that idiot Walliams that his dictionary is not complete. Oh, I just remembered, I am David Walliams. Bother!

All the horrid grown-ups – Wrath, the Envys, Pride, Sloth and the Gluttons – were all locked in cages on the deck. They rattled the bars and screamed at the sky.

"WE'LL GET YOU FOR THIS!" they cried.

"SO LONG, SUCKERS!" called out the boy.

"HA! HA!" laughed Jemima, and she, Ned and **Slime** soared high up above the clouds.

Finally, they flew towards the sun as it set on the most extraordinary day **MULCH** had ever known.

ZOOM!

Jemima held tight to her brother, wrapping her arms round his chest. The boy looked over his shoulder and smiled. No words were necessary.*

Eventually, the three returned to the clearing in the forest, landing at the spot where they had left Ned's wheelchair.

Slime turned back into its usual blobby self.

---

* *It is not because I am too lazy to write them.*

WOW!" exclaimed Jemima, her face beaming with joy.

"I know, right?" replied Ned. "WOW!"

"So my little brother is some kind of superhero now?"

Ned chuckled. "Ha! Ha! I guess so! But, you know what? I don't want to be a superhero. I just want to be me."

With that, the boy slipped off **Slime** for the last time, and back into his wheelchair.

"That's better!" said Ned. "Not nearly so slimy."

"**Well,**" began **Slime,** "**it seems as if my work here is done. I will bid you both a fond farewell.**"

The two children hugged the great slimy blob.

"Thank you, **Slime.** We will never forget you," said Ned.

"I will go and find some other children who might need naughty pranks played on grown-ups!"

"Lucky them," said Ned.

"**Look after each other.**"

we will," said the pair in unison.

With that, **Slime** changed into thousands of little blobs. These little blobs flew up past the trees and into the sky. There they floated for a few moments, before darting off in all directions over the sky.

WHOOSH!

WHOOSH!

WHOOSH!

Soon, **Slime** would be in the hands of children all over the world. Children just like you.

EPILOGUE

"We should be home in time for tea," said Ned.

"It's your birthday tomorrow!" remembered Jemima.

"I know. No surprises, please!"

"As if!" chuckled the girl. "I will run your bath!"

Ned gave his sister a look.

"With water!" she continued.

"Mmm. I almost trust you!"

Ned began turning the wheels of his wheelchair, and Jemima took the handles at the back.

"Let me give you a push," she said.

"I don't need a push. In fact, why don't you hop on?"

"Are you sure?"

"Yep! This thing is cool! Let me show you what me and my wheelchair can do!"

"All right!" replied the girl as she hopped on to a bar at the back.

Ned gathered speed.

WHIRR!

Soon they'd weaved their way out of the forest and were speeding along a country lane.

Ned knocked up the front wheels, and the pair did a wheelie!

"LOVE IT!" exclaimed Jemima.

"You've seen nothing yet!"

Then he began spinning the chair round and round.

WHIZZ!

As the pair hurtled down a hill,
they exclaimed,

"WE GOT THE

ZOOMIES!"

THE END

If you enjoyed

SLIME

you are going to love
these other books by
David Walliams!

Myrtle Meek has everything
she could possibly want.

But everything isn't enough. She wants more,
more, MORE! When Myrtle declares she
wants a FING, there's only one problem...
What *is* a FING?

At The Cruel School, the lessons are appalling, the school dinners are revolting and the teachers are terrifying.

When Larker is sent to the school, she quickly discovers this and more... a real life Megamonster.

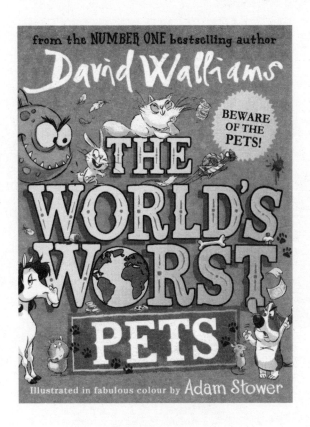

Good pets, bad pets, supervillain pets,
pets as big as a house and pets that
could eat you in one gulp – these are
the most HILARIOUS and
HORRENDOUS animals around.

MEET THE WORLD'S
WORST CHILDREN...

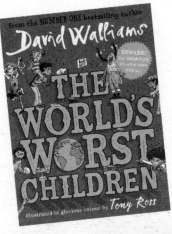
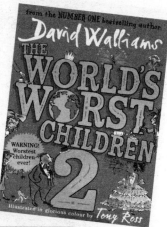

Each is nastier than the last in these
wickedly funny, deliciously
mischievous stories.

MEET THE MOST GRUESOME
GROWN-UPS EVER...

These ten tales of the world's
most spectacularly silly mums,
deliriously daft dads and splendidly
sinister teachers will leave you
rocking with laughter!

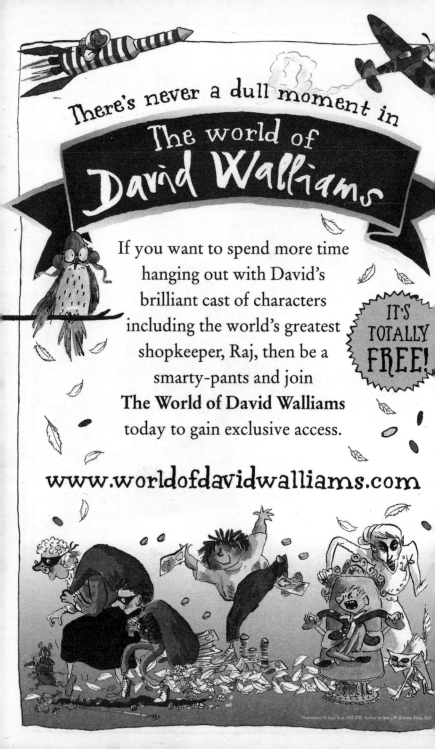